A BEAR IN A BIRDBATH

ELVA BIRCH

For my Flock. You keep me 'not writing!'

LAWN ORNAMENT SHIFTERS

Short, hilarious, and full of heart, fall in love with the quirky characters who run Wilson Kinetics, world famous artists and lawn ornament manufacturers. Shifters meet their fated mates in these clever, quick-paced stories of adventure and romance, set in a world with shifters, gnomes, and more!

The Flamingo's Fated Mate (book 1)
Gnome Sweet Gnome (book 2)
A Bear in a Birdbath (book 3)
A Garden for a Gargoyle (not that I'm writing it…)

1

BRUNO

The keen hearing of Bruno's cave bear alerted him to the interlopers, even before Anita's cheerful voice exclaimed, "Oh! Look at all the big shiny *things!*"

The factory work floor was a marvel of machines and tools, all of them kept in pristine working order. The sprawling vaulted room smelled of metal and oil, and distantly of smoke, and even the air handling system was unmarred chrome. When it was running, of course, there were metal shavings and oil rags, slag heaps and scorch marks. Workers trotted between stations, drilling and milling and grinding and shining up the mechanical lawn ornaments that were the hallmark of Wilson Kinetics. But now the space was quiet and sparkling clean, and the namesake and inspiration of the company, Frank Wilson, was touring it with his fiancé on his arm.

"Oh, Bruno!" the flamingo shifter exclaimed. "I see they got you that copper plate you wanted!"

"You could make a million pennies out of that!" the bubbly woman beside him said, staring at the solid sheet of copper on the steel form before Bruno. "No, a billion. Maybe a trillion! How much would a trillion pennies be? I'm quite good at math, believe it or not, but I have to write it down or the zeros all bounce around."

"It would be quite a lot," Frank said amiably.

"What are you going to make out of it?" Anita asked. "It's such a pretty color, and so shiny! Isn't the Statue of Liberty made of copper? It might turn green, but I like green, too. Not as much as pink, of course."

Bruno took too long to realize that she had asked him a question at the beginning of her monologue, and Frank answered for him. "A giant birdbath, probably," he said. "Bruno does exquisite metal work and I can't wait to see it."

"Did you do the one out front with the ivy and swirls? It's so beautiful and graceful! Like it's dancing! Even if it doesn't move like Frank's do."

Bruno's cave bear preened in pleasure. *Hug!* he suggested. The bear liked getting compliments and thought that the reward for every one of them should be a bone-crushing embrace.

But Frank probably wouldn't appreciate one, and he'd probably take affront if Bruno tried to hug Anita. So Bruno only grunted and ducked his head a little and probably looked like he was constipated.

"We'll lock up when we go," Frank told him. "I know you like to have the factory floor to yourself, but try not to work for the *entire* winter break."

Bruno, however, planned to do exactly that. Tobias, the gnome CEO of the company, had taken his mate off to Norway to meet his family, and Frank and Anita had tickets to a luxury resort on an island off of Costa Rica. All of the staff and mechanics had been given lush Christmas bonuses and sent home to their families for a week off, but when Frank offered to pay for a vacation for Bruno, he'd been able to imagine nothing better than having the time to create something on a grand scale without disrupting the general production schedule.

"I'll take some time off," he lied, though he had no interest in returning to his lonely bachelor apartment. "Merry Christmas."

He could hear Anita continue to exclaim over everything in the room as Frank led her out the back entrance. "All these amazing machines! So many tools! Look, a broom! What a fabulous workshop! Like Santa's, except no elves! Did I tell you that I thought of a new Christmas cupcake flavor for next year? It's gingerbread, with peppermint swirl frosting. I think that powdered sugar on top like snow would be perfect..."

Then the door finally closed behind them and Bruno breathed a sigh of relief. He liked Anita well enough, but she was a lot to take, and he liked being alone better.

No one to hug, his bear said sadly.

Bruno ignored him and got to work.

~

*B*runo shuffled back as the last echoes of the musical hammer blows faded from the empty factory floor, shifted, and surveyed his masterpiece.

The massive strikes that it took to form the cold metal required his bear's strength, and the finesse of shaping it *just right* took human sight.

He'd been working on it two days, right through the adjoining night, and was pretty sure it was nearly the following evening already. His stomach was rumbling, and he felt hollow with hunger and lack of sleep. His shoulders ached, and his hand was cramped around his hammer. His second hammer, actually; a particularly strong whack had shattered the handle of his first and favorite.

But it was worth it, when the thick plate copper finally found its rightful conformation.

This was the largest fountain tub he'd yet made. It wasn't a birdbath as much as it was an Olympic bird*pool*, big enough to sit three people, if they were friendly. Every edge was a soft leaf or a graceful flower, formed by brute force into a functional, fanciful vessel. There was a waterfall of foliage climbing one side that would hide plumbing later.

It was his masterpiece, Bruno thought. The most beautiful thing he'd ever made.

It was frivolous. Bruno didn't think that even Tobias could find a buyer willing to pay for such a monstrosity. Something for a public installment, perhaps? He had vaguely intended it for actual bathing, but he supposed it could be filled with goldfish in a lobby somewhere.

He was lucky that Frank had fronted him the cost of the giant slab of metal, without even asking what it was for.

That was the advantage of being a gazillionaire, Bruno supposed.

He peeled his aching fingers from the shaft of the hammer and set it reverently aside. He always gave a good tool the honor it deserved. His head was swimming, partly from exhaustion, partly from the euphoria of finishing.

A nap.

A nap would do him a world of good. His bear spent this time of year fighting off the urge to hibernate (and inappropriately hug people), and a rest would refresh them both.

The drive home seemed like too much, so Bruno

shifted again, climbed into his new creation, and curled into a comfortable furry lump of cave bear.

No one would bother him, during this week of closure between Christmas and New Year's. He could sleep for a day, if his hunger let him, and dream of having a warm body here with him to fill all the empty places in his heart.

2

MARGO

Margo prowled the empty bakery.

Harriet had decided to close the shop after Christmas while she went overseas with her new gnome lover, having distributed generous holiday bonuses so that everyone could enjoy a little time with their families or do some traveling.

But Margo didn't have a family outside of the other bakery employees, and she didn't have any interest in traveling.

It surprised her how much she missed the business being open. It was such a sense of satisfaction, keeping all the moving pieces in sync, knowing that she was keeping people full and happy, part of a *team*.

Trolls didn't usually take day jobs at all, but the city was cracking down on vagrants, so her usual home beneath the river bridge had been cleaned up, and she'd been kicked out. There was a well-lit bike path there now, and a lot of graffiti that she would never have tolerated. But well-mannered bridge trolls didn't have a place in the rank and file of city administration, and without a deed, she had no claim on the space. She'd been cast adrift, forced to look for a place to rent and a job to pay for it.

Harriet's bakery, Patty Cakes, had not been her first stop.

Margo had applied at the city junkyard (the dogs were afraid of her), a bodyguard service (the other bodyguards were afraid of her), and a temp agency that flatly rejected her on the basis that she wouldn't fit in standard office chairs.

"You can't expect a company to make concessions for a temporary secretary," the recruiter had said apologetically. "It's just not reasonable."

No one would want you, was the unspoken message from every one of them.

Shifters were one thing. Trolls were quite another.

Margo came upon Patty Cakes by word of mouth, because Harriet had a habit of hiring misfits and drifters and Margo realized with chagrin that she was both of those things.

"Do you have any baking experience?" Harriet asked her, eying her from toe to nose. Harriet was tall and slight, but Margo was much taller and not at all slight.

"No," Margo admitted.

"Customer service?"

Margo thought about that carefully. "In a manner of speaking. I've done…transportation oversight. Bridges, mostly."

Harriet blinked at her. "So, more like security?"

Margo stifled a sigh. It was the obvious role for her and she knew better than to be picky about employment by this point. "Yes."

"Oh," Harriet said, shaking her head. "I have all the security I need right now. What I really need is a business manager."

"To manage the business?" Margo almost salivated. She knew that trolls weren't associated with brains or organization, but she had always loved contracts and rules and making moving parts fit together.

"That *is* what a business manager does," Harriet said dryly, turning away.

Margo felt her cheeks heat. She was so tired of being underestimated. Impulsively, she caught Harriet's arm, and was surprised by the woman's unexpected strength. "Look, I'm a troll, not a politician or public speaker. But I can set up spreadsheets and organize a work shift. I know labor laws and can see three violations from your front door. I'd make sure your business was running smoothly and keep you out of trouble. No one shorts me or gives me excuses."

They looked at each other appraisingly, and Harriet finally chuckled. "You know what? I think you'll do just fine here. Let's do a month's trial and see if we can still stand each other. You might be exactly what this place needs. I've got hiring papers, do you have a mailing address?"

Margo's moment of hope froze into despair. "I'm… between places."

"I seem to have a type," Harriet snorted. "I have a spare room in the basement that is not at all cleared for residency if you don't want to be picky or legal and don't care about the damp."

Margo thought wistfully about her below-bridge abode that was a bike path now. "It sounds *perfect.*"

It was, arguably, short of perfect. There was a disaster every week, by the end of her trial month, Margo was positive that Harriet was using the business as a front for money laundering, and the staff was the surliest, most motley crew she had ever been a part of.

And Margo had never been happier.

Best of all was Eva.

Eva was as petite as Margo was monstrous, with fluffy light hair trimmed short, and big, shy blue eyes in a heart-shaped face.

Another of Harriet's obvious pity hires, the sweet, skittish woman was in Margo's ledgers as her personal assistant, but she didn't seem to do any actual administrative work. She made terrible coffee, stuttered on the phone or in the face of any visitor who spoke above a whisper, and had no idea how Harriet's file system worked.

In fact, she seemed to be working as Harriet's exclusive tailor, concocting frivolous and fancy dresses with no purpose that Margo could discern.

That was not Margo's first clue that there was something underhanded happening with Harriet's business.

"You're wondering why I need a ballgown to be a baker," Harriet said, when Margo brought in the suspect books and gave a violet velvet gown on a dressmaker dummy a long suspicious look.

"I'm wondering why we have a seventeen thousand dollar cash payment for a two hour catering job marked *Candid Cupcakes*."

"Hmm," Harriet said, pursing her lips. "That one *is* probably a little obvious."

"If you're going to be doctoring your records, you shouldn't make them that blatant," Margo said blandly. "It's just…tacky."

"You don't care what I'm really doing?" Harriet said shrewdly.

"I care that you'd do it so stupidly you drag the rest of us down with you," Margo countered. She'd lost any civic loyalty she felt when she was evicted from her ancestral bridge, but the staff of Patty Cakes had become like family.

Harriet was refreshingly honest. "Look, Nancy Drew, I steal expensive things from rich people who won't miss them, and this business is a front for laundering money and hiring people who need work because life dealt them a hard hand," Harriet said bluntly. "I understand if you have an ethical problem with that and will grant you two weeks severance if you choose to leave."

Margo spent several sleepless nights wrestling with her conscience and finally came back to Harriet's office with a counter-proposal.

"I'll be your manager, but only if you actually let me manage."

Harriet furrowed her brow and gestured for Margo to go on.

"Let me make the business solvent in actuality, not just in image, and I want to set up a retirement fund for the employees and offer better benefits and hours."

Harriet grinned dangerously. "Are you unionizing my staff?"

"Would that threaten you?" Margo growled back, even as she recognized that she was treading on dangerous ground.

Harriet only laughed in delight. "Do it, Delores!" she commanded, referencing the famous union hero, Delores Huerta. "Keep your correct ledgers and I'll keep mine, and I'll absolve you of any wrong-doing if I'm discovered. You keep the riff raff down and the staff from thinking they could take advantage of me, and I'd be sorry to lose you."

That had been the start of a long and successful partnership, and Margo was happier than she'd ever been in her life, too smart to yearn for more that she knew she couldn't have.

The bakery was quiet now, closed for the holiday between Christmas and New Year's, and Margo missed the bustle of the diverse crew in the bakery. No one was swearing in the kitchen or dropping pans. There were no customers, no bakers, no candy makers with wooden spoons going after knuckles. The only one in the whole building was Eva, two floors above, and Margo told herself she was imagining the creak on the stairs when she heard it.

Then the front door gave its cheerful alert and Margo was up from her bed to march up and see what could possibly have drawn Eva out from her cozy, quiet rooms.

3

EVA

*E*va stared at the phone. Why were they so *hard?*

Understanding the device was simple enough. A number called a person, the commands were obvious, she listened here and spoke there. But knowing what to *say* was the hard part. Gathering up the courage to dial and to then have a conversation with someone that she couldn't see and get social cues from...it was a kind of torture.

Her shoulder blades *itched.*

But debts mattered, to her more than most, and she had one to pay off. She held the phone at arm's length and pushed the connection button while holding her breath, as if it was a hand grenade or can of biscuits under pressure.

"Antonio," the voice said at the other end.

"It's Eva," she said, too quietly, and she had to repeat herself into the phone when he couldn't hear her. "You-your message, it said you had a job for m-me."

"Right! I've got an opportunity for you to buy out the rest of your debt."

Eva felt like she was holding her breath and made

herself try to breath normally, which only made her pant. "I can't steal from Harriet!" she blurted. "I can't do it!"

"Chill, sister," Antonio said easily. "I'm looking at a bigger payout than Harriet's petty thefts at this point. I need you to break into Wilson Kinetics."

"The lawn ornament factory?" Eva was confused. "You want me to steal lawn ornaments?"

Antonio laughed, though Eva hadn't meant to be funny. "I want the plans for next year's sculpture. Flamingo billionaire Frank Wilson has rivals that want to scoop him with cheap knockoffs. All you have to do is figure out what he's going to unveil next year."

Eva chewed on her lip. "I don't know how to do that."

"I've got the building codes," Antonio said. "I'll text them to you. All you have to do is waltz right in and snoop through his files. I know that cabinet locks won't slow you down, with your faery tricks, and if you're caught, nothing connects us."

"Will there be guards?"

"A skeleton crew at most."

Eva hoped he didn't mean literal skeletons. "I guess…"

"That's my girl!"

Eva did not like the idea of being his girl. She would never be anyone's *girl* again. But she was willing to *snoop* if it meant her freedom.

~

*E*va's car had been untouched in the bakery parking lot so long that it was buried in snow.

She stared at the lump, trying to remember which direction she'd parked it. Was that the front of the sedan? She shivered and went back in for a broom from the bakery.

The first sweep she made fell directly into her boots, causing her to curse and stomp around miserably. Her arms weren't long enough, even with the broom, to get all the way over the car, but after several minutes of struggle, she had uncovered enough of it to get the door open.

Eva held her breath as she started it, and sighed gratefully when it reluctantly caught, coughing and groaning in protest. The glass on every window frosted up immediately, and Eva turned the heater on full and got out to clear off more snow so she wouldn't be a hazard in traffic.

Not that there was much traffic.

Most people were home with their families, and the recent snow meant the roads were slushy and perilous. Eva navigated slowly, consulting the directions on her phone at each intersection.

Following her instructions to the letter, she parked at the side of a busy bar, where her car would be unremarkable, except for the snow mohawk that hadn't fully blown off on her slow journey through town. When all the mid-holiday drinkers were safely out of the parking lot and in the bright-lit bar, Eva got out of her car and trudged in the opposite direction for a block.

She pushed the hood of her coat back, wincing at the noise the slippery synthetic fabric made in the quiet night, and squinted at the warehouse. The lot in front of Wilson Kinetics was brightly lit and had not been cleared since Christmas at least. The only car was one sad SUV so covered in snow that it was little more than a lump.

Eva felt sorry for the driver who was going to have to uncover it and wiggled her cold, damp toes in her boots.

The snow was a soft, plush carpet over everything, and there were no tracks in or out. If there were any security rounds, they had been by before the last snowfall. Did that mean that they were due for a sweep? Or was everything particularly lax in the window between Christmas and New Year's?

Eva would have preferred to bide her time and surveil the warehouse for a few days to figure out the timing of any guards, but the holiday opportunity was a fleeting thing, and Antonio had not given her a choice.

She looked behind her at the trail she was leaving from where she'd parked her car and winced. It was painfully obvious, a slash of shadow through the unbroken white. She was the worst thief in the history of the world.

Eva was careful with her next steps, but she no longer had the ability to float on top of the snow, so there was little she could do to mask her path.

Eva was focused so hard on trying to keep more snow from over-topping her boots that she was surprised to find herself at the door at last. Keenly aware of the bright lights and her unstealthy red coat, knowing anyone who looked might see her, she scrambled at the lock of the door, then froze as a car rumbled by on the quiet, unplowed road.

They passed without pausing, possibly on their way to the very bar that Eva had just left.

Her key opened the lock, the code she'd been given turned off the alarm system, and Eva breathed a short-lived sigh of relief.

4

MARGO

Margo frowned at the footsteps in the snow. Eva had paused here, clearly, and then gone on.

Did she know that Margo was following her, or was this just general caution? Margo didn't need a trail to know that Eva was headed towards the deserted Wilson Kinetics factory; it was the only thing on this stretch of road besides the bar behind her where Eva had parked her car.

Margo frowned through the gently falling snow at the bright-lit building. Was that door slightly ajar?

She was wading forward through the uncleared snow before common sense could stop her.

The door opened at her touch; Eva had taped the door latch open, and the security pad just inside had been disarmed. Margo set the door back the way she'd found it, shut but not latched, and paused to let her eyes adjust to the dark.

A hand-lettered sign with a giant pink lawn flamingo wearing a helicopter hat hung in greeting. "Welcome back, Flock!" it said.

Past a secretary's cluttered desk, there were doors to offices and a hallway that ended with industrial double doors that suggested a large space beyond. Margo heard a rustling sound through those doors, and she crept towards them carefully, peering into each room she passed.

Was Eva stealing something? Frank Wilson was known for his huge jeweled sculptures, so there were probably gems and precious metals somewhere here. There might also be industry secrets worth pilfering. The company itself was a multi-billion dollar business, thanks to the CEO genius of Harriet's new beau, Tobias Underhill, but it wasn't a direct retail site; Margo couldn't imagine that they had vast amounts of cash on hand.

And she also couldn't imagine Eva *stealing*.

Eva was the sweetest, gentlest woman that Margo had ever met, as innocent as an angel. She jumped at loud noises and stammered whenever someone spoke too loudly. Even Harriet tempered her sharp tongue around the shy seamstress.

It was also obvious to anyone with a lick of sense that she was in some kind of trouble. She always wore a hood up in public and never met anyone's eyes unless she was startled into it. She didn't leave Harriet's bakery if she didn't have to.

Margo had tried to coax her story out of her only once, one evening that she found an excuse to go upstairs to Harriet's private office, where Eva lived in the back. Eva's haunted blue eyes had undone whatever was left of Margo's heart, and she had never asked about Eva's past again.

Margo had reached the end of the hallway, where big fire doors were closed.

The double doors had windows, and Margo looked through into a huge work room, filled with equipment. She recognized lathes, drills, and enormous milling machines. Most of the workstations were dark, still, and meticulously clean, but one work table, halfway across the space, was brightly lit and littered with shards of metal and broken tools.

There was no sign of movement, but Margo heard the snick of a lock somewhere down the hall behind her.

For a split second, she thought it was Eva, but she realized that there was no effort being made at stealth, and there were two male voices talking.

"It's just Bruno," one of them said. "Don't startle him while he's working."

"I'm not even sure why we have this job. A thief would run into him and just give right up."

"I told you, this job is cake. Who's going to rob Wilson Kinetics? Best-loved billionaire in the world. It would be like kicking puppies."

"Let's just do a sweep of the work floor and get back to our game."

A sweep of the work floor. Margo realized that the voices were coming her way, and she needed a place to hide, immediately. It was too late to get back down the hallway; the only way out was forward, so she eased one of the double doors open and slipped out to the factory floor to find a place big enough for her to hide—which was not going to be the easiest thing given the fact that she was six foot and some spare inches, and as broad-shouldered as a linebacker in the orc league.

For a moment, she hoped that she could simply keep one of the bigger pieces of equipment between herself and the guards. Unfortunately, the two guards split up, clearly intending to sweep either side of the room and cut their job in half. The lines of their flashlights crisscrossed and Margo crept further in, trying to find anything that might be big enough to hide in as she cursed their thoroughness.

The solution was obvious at once. There was a huge hammered copper basin, edged in flowers and fancy leaves, sitting in the center of the lit workspace. This was clearly the masterpiece that was the cause of the mess. Margo timed her advance, moving when the guards were both looking up into the catwalks and she took two long steps to dive into it.

Unfortunately, it was already occupied.

She thought it was a sleeping buffalo at first, thick-furred and well-padded, then it rolled and wrapped strong arms around her.

A bear? If it was, it was the biggest bear that Margo had ever seen. She was too startled to fight, and still in stealth mode, and then the figure shifted beneath her into a massive man.

5

BRUNO

*B*runo was dreaming of snow and saunas, the surreal contrast of cold and searing heat both exciting and tantalizing.

This dream was interrupted by the sudden crushing weight of a very large figure dropping down on top of him in the tub and he shifted in his sleep.

Instinctively, he rolled to grapple with the interloper, which was when he realized that it was very definitely a woman. He had a large, soft breast in one hand, and a haunch of shapely hip in the other.

"What was that?"

Bruno came awake enough to remember that he was in his own copper creation, and recognized the voice of one the factory guards. As he woke, he realized that the fascinating creature he was clutching must have dived on top of him to avoid their attention.

"I didn't hear anything, what was it?"

"I don't know. Kind of a thunk? Like a sack of flour falling over or something."

"Pretty sure there aren't any sacks of flour in here," the other said sarcastically.

The sack-of-flour woman lying on top of him was still and stiff, and Bruno was appalled to realize that he too was very, *very* stiff as he held equally still. She wasn't volunteering to sit up and get away from him, but she must realize what she had fallen onto; it was not small enough to be something in his pocket. He was still holding her breast, as well, and his fingers were unconsciously kneading at it.

Hug! Bruno's bear insisted. *Hug!*

Bruno's bear thought that bone-crushing hugs were an appropriate way to greet anyone and Bruno often had to hold him back from embracing cashiers and strangers on the street...but he thought that this might be a more fitting opportunity.

"There's no one here," the first guard said firmly. "Let's swing by the mess hall and get a coffee."

Bruno lay still until the doors outside clicked shut and the woman on top of him scrambled off his cock and out of his grip, but she didn't get out of the tub.

"You're not Eva," she said in a growl as they untangled their limbs and she got as far away from him in the tub as she could.

Bruno kind of wished he *was* Eva, the way she said the name. "I'm afraid not," he agreed, sitting up slowly and offering his hand. "Bruno Bigliotti, at your...ah...service." Then he got a look into her face and the fluttering feeling in his chest that he'd thought was just the lingering tail of his dream solidified into an iron certainty.

Mate! his cave bear roared in triumph. *Mine!*

The stranger was a woman nearly as tall and as broad as Bruno himself, which was unusual in most men and unheard of in women. She had soft waves of deep brown hair and a face with strong planes and huge brown eyes. Her lips were slightly parted, as if she was puzzled.

"I'm—" She stopped short of giving her name at the last moment. "Why didn't you turn me in?"

Mine! his cave bear growled.

"You didn't seem to want to be found," Bruno said simply. "And I didn't want to *share* you." The tub was just small enough that he didn't have to lean forward very far in order to cover her tantalizing mouth with his own.

He felt the moment her surprise gave way to surrender, and then when she seemed to reconsider and went from kissing him back to shoving him away.

That sequence was long enough to raise his desire from sizzling to absolutely desperate, and it caused almost physical pain when she struggled away from him and out of the tub, to fall on the ground with a crash. "Wait!" he cried, but she was up and scrambling for the door much faster than a woman of her size ought to be able to move.

"Wait!" he called again, but then she was through the doors and gone and Bruno was still trying to figure out all of his limbs and get out of the birdbath.

6

EVA

$\mathcal{E}$va blessed her small size as the flashlights swept harmlessly over her hiding place, and it was only a few moments before she could creep out and resume her mission.

She heard some commotion from the factory floor that made her pause, but that wasn't her objective.

Frank Wilson's office was near the front, and it was a comfortable, sprawling room with couches and bean bags. It wasn't as ostentatious as Eva expected. There was a popcorn machine, and a cooler full of drinks. A number of flamingo statues cluttered his desk.

Antonio had told her that security would be minimal once she was in, but Eva still moved into the room cautiously. There were guards on rotation and she didn't want to catch their attention.

The file cabinet by the desk was locked, but Eva had no problem opening it; faery lock picks were foolproof.

The filing *system*, on the other hand…

Eva thought that the first folder being labeled "Accounting" was a good start with the alphabet, but the next one was marked "Finances" and then "Fashion," followed by "Zoo Project" and "Other Stuff." It wasn't that she had expected a folder conveniently labeled "Next Year's Project," but it would have been nice.

After a frustrated exhale, Eva started rifling through folders.

The tabs were just the start of Frank's thorough disorganization. Within "Accounting" were receipts (to be expected), reviews (perhaps misfiled?), and love letters to Anita, which Eva paused to read despite herself.

"My darling baker love,

You are sweeter than any of your confections,

like sugar and chocolate.

My tongue craves you.

Your skin is better than icing.

And best of all is your laugh,

infectious like a head cold,

but twice as much fun."

The spacing implied poetry, but Eva couldn't make it scan or rhyme and she gave up after a few pages. She put the letters back in the folder where she'd found them and told herself that she didn't want anyone writing such drivel for her.

Such *tender* drivel. Eva wasn't sure how she would feel about being compared to a virus, but Frank's sincerity was clear.

She shoved aside her weak moment of yearning and went to the next folder. Somewhere, hopefully she would find the document she was searching for.

What she wasn't looking for was company, but company found her anyway.

When the door to the office popped open, Eva had a moment of terror that turned to relief. Eva would know that silhouette anywhere, with its familiar, trustworthy muscle and that particular length of arm and leg. It was a form with curves in all the proper places for snuggling up against, strong and safe.

It wasn't a security guard, it was Margo.

"What are you doing here?" Eva hissed, before she could stop herself.

"I should ask *you* that," Margo growled back.

Margo's growls were never terrifying. It was more like a kitten purring. "I-I-" Eva looked around. She'd been caught breaking into not only Wilson Kinetics, but Frank Wilson's personal files. "It's just that… well, it's kind of a long story."

"Eva, I don't know what kind of trouble you're in…" Margo's voice was low and gentle. She had come around the desk.

"I'm getting myself *out* of trouble," Eva protested. She didn't want Margo to think she was helpless and weak. Margo, of *all* people.

"This looks like you're digging yourself deeper into trouble," Margo snapped. "You can't just break into Wilson Kinetics!"

Had she disappointed Margo? All of Eva's troubles seemed to crash down onto her and she felt her eyes fill with tears.

No.

Eva wasn't sure if it was pride or fear that drove her. She was grateful that the room was too dark for Margo to witness her frailty, and mad at herself for being so awful at everything. "You shouldn't have followed me!" she cried. "I don't want you here! You're going to ruin *everything*!"

7

MARGO

argo flinched, surprised and dismayed by Eva's unexpected anger. "I know that you're in some kind of a mess and I wanted to protect you!" she protested. It was more clear than ever that Eva was in over her head.

"I d-don't need your protection!" Eva said, looking fearlessly up at Margo. "I can fight my own battles!"

"I've watched you lose a fight with a trash bag!" Margo hissed impatiently. "Will you keep your voice down and *stop being so mulish?*"

"I'm not *mulish*," Eva sputtered in outrage. "You're just sticking your nose where it doesn't belong! You should never have followed me!!"

Margo knew a lost cause when she saw one, and she knew that her own powers of persuasion were unequal to Eva's unexpected resolve. She might not be able to convince Eva to leave quietly, but she did have one option left.

"What are you doing?" Eva gasped, when Margo stooped to take her by the waist. "How dare you!"

She was even lighter than she looked, and she was so surprised by Margo's move that it was no harder than hefting a chicken to her shoulder.

A chicken that immediately began to fight her.

Eva was not that strong, compared to Margo, but she was slippery, and distractingly lithe, and it was like trying to hold onto a greased-up eel. A greased-up eel with little fists and feet that hammered at Margo's shoulders. A curvy, *sexy* little greased-up eel whose struggles were stirring Margo into a whirlwind of confused emotion and distracted longing. Margo had been right to avoid touching her for so long.

"I'm not letting you—ow!—get yourself caught trying to burgle Wilson Kinetics for some—ow!—hare-brained reason when there are other choices!"

"I don't have another choice!" Eva hissed, finally squirming from Margo's grasp as she wedged a foot against Margo's collarbone.

Margo twisted desperately to catch her before she could fall to the unforgiving floor, and suddenly had Eva in her arms, close against her.

"You could ask for help," Margo whispered.

Eva was still at last, staring back up at her with galaxy-deep eyes filled with longing.

"You're my friend," Margo said haltingly. "Probably my best friend. I'd…do anything you asked."

"My *friend?*"

Margo tried to identify her tone. Was it only that she was grateful and surprised that Margo considered herself a friend? Or did she yearn for something more, as Margo herself did?

On any other day, she would have released Eva without presuming further liberty, sure that no one could want advances from a monster such as herself. But on any other day, she hadn't been kissed breathless by a complete stranger in a waterless decorative pond, and there was already a fire in her belly that hungered for fuel.

She bent down and put her lips to Eva's.

8

———————

EVA

The first time that Eva met Margo, she'd been filled with an unexpected sense of safety.

She knew that the other employees of Harriet's bakery were terrified of the huge woman, and that she ought to be, too. Margo was a hulking monster of a matriarch, and there was no warmth to her demeanor or invitation in her manner. She ruled the bakery with an iron fist and brooked no nonsense.

And Eva, of all people, expected to feel threatened by her unquestioned power and grim facade.

But Margo's dominion was unfalteringly fair and beneath her growls, her strength was tempered with softness. She never spoke loudly if it was not necessary, and her touch was always gentle.

With Eva, she seemed especially careful, and Eva was sure that her kindness was never less than genuine.

She was not a particularly handsome woman, with a heavy jaw and a broad forehead, but Eva had plenty of experience with beautiful things and knew the value of meaningless pretty words and empty promises. Margo had lovely warm eyes and clever fingers, and Eva found her face interesting rather than off-putting.

They had come to what Eva considered a cautious understanding under Harriet's roof. Margo lived in the basement, Eva lived in the upstairs back office, and they shared the communal space. Neither of them was given to a great deal of random chatter to fill the space, but they found common ground in disparaging Harriet's musical choices and changing the soundtrack the moment she left. Eva introduced her to Faery Metal, and Margo broadened her mind to jazz and ginlark.

Margo often brought little gifts from the bakery up with her, and Eva mended her clothes and added little embellishments of embroidery. Subtle decoration, because Margo herself was so understated, but Eva enjoyed knowing that Margo was wearing a touch of her own creation at her wrist and collar.

Eva had never let herself imagine there might be more between them than this simple, undefined friendship.

Not until Margo kissed her.

Suddenly, there was electricity under all of her skin and she was on fire from her toes to the top of her head, and all she wanted was Margo's touch and the warmth of her arms.

So when Margo kissed her, Eva kissed her back.

She was so strong, soft, and *safe*. Eva couldn't understand how the meeting of their mouths could be both exciting and so comfortable at the same time. This was home. It was belonging and craving and calming, all at once.

Eva didn't want to analyze why Margo might kiss her, she only wanted to enjoy it, to lean into the beautiful moment and make the most of it.

So it was very annoying when there was suddenly a

noise at the doorway, and Margo released Eva very abruptly and turned to find something to throw at a dark figure filling the doorframe.

The closest thing to hand was a massive pink marble flamingo statue. Margo picked it up effortlessly and hurled it at the interloper.

9

BRUNO

Bruno considered himself a reasonably intelligent man. He knew he wasn't brilliant, like Tobias, or as wildly charismatic as Frank, but besides banging out some decent art, he could balance his own finances and hold up his end of most conversations.

He was not exactly proving his mental capacity now.

The marble flamingo that came flying at him when he entered Frank's office was the first distraction.

Shifter reflexes helped him duck the missile (it was more aerodynamic than most actual flamingos) and it hit the wall behind him and broke into three jagged pieces.

Frank is going to kill someone for that, Bruno thought.

But the second distraction was his cave bear in his head.

For the most part, his cave bear was a quiet companion. He mostly wanted to hug people, nap, and stuff himself on sweets, keeping his conversation to single words of suggestion. But now, he was like a one-bear brass band in Bruno's head, repeating the same line of music at maximum volume.

Our mates! Our mates! Our mates!

The Amazon who had taken shelter in the birdbath with him was the catapult of the stone flamingo, and she was even more breathtaking at her full height and bristling protectiveness.

Behind her was a crouching figure that would have been tiny even without the foil of the other woman, surrounded by a pile of open folders, a flashlight on the floor casting them into sharp shadows. Was that Frank's awful *poetry*?

Our mates! Our mates! Our mates!

It was impossible to think around his cave bear's triumphant caterwauling.

"Eva, get *out* of here!" The woman he'd kissed was casting around for something else to throw at him. Frank's desk was full of unfortunate fodder. A plush flamingo dog toy squeaked off of Bruno's shoulder.

"I can't go yet!" Eva was wildly tossing folders aside. "*You* go!"

Our mates! Our mates! Our mates!

Bruno realized that he should be reassuring them that he wasn't going to hurt them. He knew that he was a terrifying brute of a man, and the room was dark. But when he tried to form words around his cave bear's litany, it only came out, "Owl ates! Primates! Too late!"

Our mates! Our mates! Our mates!
Will you please shut up so I can make real words?
Our mates! Our mates! Our mates!
Which one?
HUG THEM!

What did that even *mean*? He thought that the flamingo-flinging woman was his mate, but was it possible that the slight figure behind her was *as well*?

His cave bear was certainly convinced.

Our mates! Our mates! Our mates!

Will you stop that?!

The first woman was advancing on him now, clearly invested in protecting her companion. "We have to get out of here!" she called back over her shoulder.

"I'll let you go!" Bruno tried to say, but his cave bear wanted no part of that, and he found himself wrestling his own inner animal so that the words came out, "Highlight Lego!"

She was in grappling range now, and Bruno was distracted by the idea of hand-to-hand, remembering the feel of her generous breast under his fingers. "Plato amigo!" he tried again.

Our mates! Our mates! Our mates!

"You can't go!"

Of all the words to get right, those were the wrong ones.

The woman bearing down on him clearly took that as a threat, and she reached for the nearest weapon at hand.

It was Frank's vintage popcorn machine.

10

EVA

"You knocked him out!" Eva exclaimed, abandoning her pilfered papers to ensure that Margo hadn't killed the poor man.

The man who had filled the doorway with his horrifying—and yet oddly not at all horrifying—form lay stretched out face down on the floor with the broken parts of the popcorn machine all around him. Eva tried in vain to turn him over to assess him for injury. He'd have a headache, for sure.

"Well, you weren't willing to leave, and I couldn't exactly fight him *and* football carry you out of here at the same time," Margo snarled back. "You're slippery!"

Despite the gravity of the moment—they'd just been caught red-handed in the act of trespassing and attempted theft and knocked out some poor brute wearing a Wilson Kinetics badge—Eva's brain got stuck on the idea of what, exactly, was slippery right now.

She shook her head. "You don't understand," she wailed. "This isn't your problem."

"It could be," Margo insisted. "If you'd trust your *friends*."

Friends.

Kissing friends? Eva's lips still burned with need but neither of them seemed willing to speak of it. Did Margo *regret* it?

Eva gave up trying to roll the man over. He had a strong, steady pulse, at least, and was breathing. "I'm sorry you got dragged into this," she explained reluctantly. "I have…some debt to pay off, and a guy I know sent me to find Frank Wilson's plans for next year's sculpture so that a rival company can beat them to the punch with a line of knock-offs."

"I didn't realize that lawn ornaments were such a cutthroat business. Did you find it?"

"I don't know that there's anything here," Eva said in despair. "It's mostly bad love poetry and cupcake recipes."

Margo signed in defeat. "I'll…I'll help you look. It will go faster with two sets of hands."

She turned on the overhead light, which did a much better job of illuminating the files than Eva's flashlight, and if their pitched battle hadn't drawn the guards, probably the light wouldn't, either.

Margo nudged the man out of the way so that she could close the door.

It was much faster to go through the files with Margo, but if Frank had made notes about the next sculpture, neither of them had any luck finding them. There were copies of flyers for extravagant staff picnics and blank employee of the month certificates, ticket stubs for the zoo, and program books from comedy events. Frank had notes about Anita, a draft of a best man's speech for Tobias, shopping lists, and a lot of things that made no sense, like

"Winged gorilla mud wrestling." (His handwriting was also very terrible.)

Eva took photographs of some of the most indecipherable parts.

"Will that work?" Margo wanted to know.

"I don't know," Eva admitted. "I've done what I was asked, so maybe it will be enough."

There was a groan from the man Margo had knocked out and they went to make sure he was still sleeping. Margo rolled him effortlessly over, and Eva could see his face for the first time in the bright light.

He was incredibly handsome, with one of those chiseled movie-star faces edged in neatly trimmed facial hair. "That's Bruno Bigliotti. He makes those fancy birdbaths that win art awards. He's a cave bear shifter."

Eva looked up in time to catch Margo blushing as she knelt to check his pulse. She was *blushing!* Well, no wonder. The man was an absolute beauty, even if he was a huge brute. Eva returned her gaze to him so that she wouldn't stare longingly at Margo and disturb the fragile truce they had right now.

"Mate," he murmured. "You're my mate…"

Eva and Margo both froze and exchanged an astonished glance over his head.

Margo was this man's mate?

Eva told herself that there was no reason for her bolt of jealousy. She didn't even know the terrifying man, and she didn't have a claim on either of these people.

"Let's get out of here before he wakes up and calls in reinforcements," Margo advised sensibly.

11

MARGO

argo anxiously watched the papers for an entire week before she let herself believe that they'd gotten away scot-free.

There was no news about a break in at Wilson Kinetics, and no report of one of their high-profile Chief Operating Officers being found knocked out with a popcorn machine broken over his head. There was no mention of thieves being caught on tape or evidence of any misdemeanors.

No one came to Harriet's bakery with an arrest warrant, and no investigators stopped by with innocent questions like 'Where were you at midnight on December 28th?'

Eva was safe.

Safe from persecution, at least. Antonio seemed satisfied with the pictures that Eva had sent him. At least, he didn't seem to be pressing her about her hanging debt, or talking her into further industrial espionage.

But Eva wasn't safe to *Margo* now.

Margo's crush had been buried so deep that she barely

recognized it herself, and now it was out in the unflattering light. Eva was out of Margo's league. She was someone else's *mate*. And yet Margo couldn't stop *wanting* her.

Margo prowled the bakery more diligently than ever, and probably scared off more sales than she secured. She caught herself scowling for no reason, only realizing what she was doing when someone burst into tears or started stammering apologies.

She didn't see much of Eva because she avoided Harriet's second floor office unless she was directly summoned for some reason.

When they met, briefly, in the hall, or in the kitchen after hours, their conversation was badly stilted and they hung to opposite sides of the stainless steel counters even when it was obviously what they were doing. They escaped every encounter as quickly as possible.

Margo had ruined *everything*.

One impulsive, unwelcome kiss, and she'd shattered their fragile friendship.

She couldn't stop thinking about what Eva had felt like in her arms, the soft, warmth of her, and the flutter of her lips as they kissed. She convinced herself that Eva hadn't really kissed her back. It was just a reflex, a moment so keen in Margo's memory that she'd exaggerated what really happened.

Because she saw how Eva looked down at Bruno when he was asleep. And she was his *mate*.

Two kisses in one night, both of them just a tease at what might have been, and all of her opportunities overwhelmed and washed away when they met *each other*.

Margo was thrilled for them at the same time that she despaired for herself, because how could she be so selfish as to deny them that shred of happiness she briefly thought might have been her own?

But Margo couldn't have either of them, there was no point in pining, and if she wanted to remove the horrible complication that Eva had become, there was *one* thing she could do. If Eva wasn't going to willingly follow up on her mate, Margo wasn't going to wait for the factory head to send out a glass slipper or an invitation to a ball to find his escaped princess.

"You want to set Eva up with *who?*" Harriet had mellowed considerably since she met Tobias and agreed to marry him, but she still had her sharp wit and suspicious mind. *"Why?"*

"They met unexpectedly while you were away and… ah…hit it off," Margo said between clenched teeth. "I think they'd make a cute couple."

"I never took you for a matchmaker," Harriet said, twisting the ring on her finger. "But don't think that I didn't notice when you let Tobias up to my office that first time."

The way Harriet said his name was soft and lingering. She seemed to hear herself, stopped playing with her rough diamond, and frowned at Margo. "You don't think she'll get hurt, do you?"

Even the distant possibility of it gave Margo a pang of worry and regret. "He wouldn't dare," she snarled. She forced herself to gentle her voice. "I think they'll be great together," she said. "She's…his mate."

Harriet's whole face lit up. "Really? Oh, that's wonderful!" She seemed to hear herself. "What is *wrong* with me?" She shook her head in disgust. "So, why do I need to set them up if that's the case? Why aren't they off nesting already? These things usually work themselves out without interference."

"They met in…slightly weird circumstances." *He was*

unconscious, and she was tossing Wilson Kinetics. "They didn't get to the point of exchanging names."

If Harriet had any suspicions that Margo secretly wanted Eva—or Bruno—*and* Bruno!—for herself, she gave no indication. "I'll set something up," she promised. "Tobias is a hopeless busybody, and this will get him off of my back about the wedding for a while." She gave her ring another of those soft smiles, like she didn't really mind Tobias's various pressures.

"Thank you," Margo growled. "Now, I have some concerns about your lease contract that I wanted to bring up…"

She suspected that her hire was an act of pity because job opportunities for trolls were not thick on the ground, but when Harriet had appointed her as a manager, Margo took it seriously. She spent her evenings studying law and researching contract language, following current legal issues and poring over case studies. She took online business classes and got a subscription to The Economist. She memorized the food safety guidelines.

If anything, it only made her more boring.

Not only was she a troll, she was a *pedantic* troll, quoting regulations and enforcing the rules.

But trolls had hearts, and she'd lost hers twice now. The best she could do was mend someone else's.

1 2

EVA

The note on Eva's dress dummy had been brief. "You are required to attend a private dinner. Formal attire." An address finished the note.

It was Harriet's handwriting, and there were no clues as to the occasion, or why Eva herself was being pressed into attending. Harriet didn't often bring her to events and Eva was glad of it. The baker-thief was making noises about Eva setting up her own clothing design company, but Eva balked at the idea of having to be even a token front for such a business. Cameras flashing in her face? Interviews? No, she wanted no part of that kind of fame.

But she was intrigued by the note, and she owed Harriet a great deal, so she picked the most formal attire she had, a slight black velvet dress embroidered all over in silky black thread so that it looked rather plain until the light hit it and brought out all of the designs.

It reminded her of Margo, and Margo's kiss as she smoothed it down over her slim figure.

Why had Margo kissed her? Why did she pretend she hadn't?

Eva was jealously glad that Margo seemed disinclined to follow up on Bruno's declaration that he was her mate. Maybe the blow to his head had just addled him. It was easier to think of that, than of losing Margo to that gorgeous man.

But in some ways, it seemed like she had already lost Margo. They barely spoke now, and Margo never smiled, more stone-faced than ever. Eva could only guess why things seemed to have gone so wrong.

It was *Eva's* fault. Her heart was flawed. She was *poison*.

Eva hadn't meant to fall in love with Margo. But Margo was so kind and smart behind her gruff exterior that Eva had liked and trusted her at once, barely noticing when trust melted into affection, and at some point attraction. And then Margo had kissed her and unleashed all the tender feelings that Eva was most afraid of. Eva gritted her teeth and pulled on a coat.

The address took her to the arboretum. She pulled into the empty parking lot and gazed in confusion at the entrance. Were those rose petals scattered in the snow?

For a moment, Eva had a stab of hope and fear. Was this some form of troll courtship? Had the kiss meant something after all?

But Margo had a *mate*, and this didn't look at all like Margo's style. Eva followed the trail through the double doors, down a candle-lit hallway into the romantically lit arboretum with its arched glass ceilings.

It wasn't Margo waiting for her.

The light wasn't much more flattering, but the big man that Margo had knocked out was much less terrifying sitting at a white-clothed table holding a delicate crystal goblet in one meaty hand.

Bruno Bigliotti. The factory manager of Wilson Kinetics.

Bruno put his glass down at her approach and gingerly stood, clutching at the napkin in his lap before it could fall to the floor.

"Don't go!" he cried, and Eva realized that she was poised to flee back the way that she'd come. "I won't hurt you!"

Eva was sure that if he could arrange something like this, she would not be able to get away with something so simple as running away anyway, so she walked bravely forward.

He gazed down at her as she came close, and he was so tall—and she was so short—that she had to crane up and up to see into his face.

Eva had been enspelled before, forced to love and adore, and she was puzzled now, because this was so like this…and so completely different.

Bruno was *fascinatingly* manly. He was broad-shouldered and beautiful, and he smelled like musk and metal. He had shaved clean for this meeting, but it didn't make him look young or naïve. Eva somehow knew that he was safe and reliable, and he was undeniably attractive.

She was drawn to him, but it was not like the insidious love spell that had threatened to destroy her soul. This was not control, it was certainty. She knew beyond any shadow of doubt that this man could make her happier than she'd ever been in her life…but only if she let him.

How did she resolve this with him being *Margo's* mate? Was it only because she loved Margo that she could sense the *goodness* of this man? Was it some lingering magic that had been dormant in her heart?

"I'm Bruno," he said, offering her one of his hands.

"Eva," she breathed, when she remembered her name. His handshake was one of the gentlest things Eva had ever felt, and he let go before she could feel trapped.

He held her chair for her and a waiter melted out of the surrounding greenery to put a fresh salad at her place.

"So, I guess we sort of met, a few weekends ago," Eva finally said, when Bruno offered no conversation, looking for all the world as if he felt as awkward about this as she did. There was no use trying to pretend, and the salad didn't last long.

"You were tossing Frank's office at Wilson Kinetics."

"To be fair, Mar—my *friend* did most of the tossing," Eva corrected him. "But I was the one who broke in." If this was some elaborate attempt to get Margo in trouble, she wasn't going to fall for it.

Bruno gave a laugh. "She has an amazing arm," he said, reaching up to rub the back of his head.

He had amazing arms.

"Wha-What's all this about?" Eva had to ask. If he wasn't trying to trap Margo, maybe he wanted information about her for other reasons. Did he think that she could give him tips for courting her or catching her? Eva was hopelessly lost.

"Tobias set this up," Bruno said. "I never pictured him as such a matchmaker, but I had no idea who either of you were, or how to find you."

"I'm sorry. For breaking in. And wrecking the place up. And assaulting you."

"It meant I met the two of you," Bruno said without regret.

Eva's salad bowl was replaced by a steaming plate of gourmet pasta while she was staring at her lap. "Oh, thank you?" The waiter vanished before she could make shy eye contact.

A steak was placed before Bruno, so thick and juicy that it was on its own platter.

Dinner was a traditional framework for dates. Eating

was supposed to give her something to do, and inane comments about how delicious her meal was ought to flow effortlessly into intimate conversation about favorite foods. Instead, Eva dropped her fork, nearly fell off her chair picking it up, and then tried to eat with it before a scandalized waiter could come and bring her a new one.

Bruno seemed to be faring no better, sawing at his meat with a knife too delicate or dull for his fare, muttering under his breath. Eva thought she heard him say, "Not hugging," but it might have been "Snort muggings."

She ought to say something witty. "Noodles are funny," she blurted. "Even the name is funny. Nooo-dles." She winced. That was not even *close* to witty.

"Your friend, what was her name?"

There it was. He *was* on a fact-finding date for Margo. Because Margo was his mate.

The sauce that had a bite ago been as good as any meal Eva had ever eaten went tasteless in her mouth. "Margo," she said faintly.

"Margo." Bruno said it with approval, like he was tasting it in his mouth. "She kissed like a Margo."

"Wait, you *kissed* her?" Eva didn't understand anything that was happening. Margo had kissed *her*, she thought jealously.

"Kissed her, nearly molested her. Got knocked out by her with a popcorn machine. I spent maybe five total minutes in her company, and we've already done a lot."

"She didn't tell me that part," Eva said, trying to force herself to be happy for Margo. Everything he said only made things more complicated.

"Do you know about mates?" Bruno asked, his growly voice more growly than ever.

Eva wasn't sure how to identify what was happening in

her heart. Was it hope? Heartbreak? Longing? "Margo is your mate," she said faintly.

Even though it wasn't a question, the answer was exactly what she had dreaded, so gruff that it was barely a word: "Yes."

Eva closed her eyes and told herself that she could be happy for them. She wouldn't get either of them for herself, but she was a big enough person, emotionally if not physically, to be satisfied with the fact that they'd found each other. She just had to let go of them both.

But Bruno wasn't finished. "And you are, too."

Eva's eyes flew open. "That's a *thing*?" Her irrational attraction had a *reason*? She felt dismayed and excited and dangerously hopeful, all at once.

"Apparently," Bruno said with a shrug and a crooked smile. "I'm as surprised as you are."

It explained so much. She hadn't once been afraid of Bruno, not even when he was looming in the dark of Frank Wilson's office. She had known even then that he was no threat to her, that he could never hurt or betray her. Because he was her mate, and mates recognized each other at a level that defied logic and transcended magic.

And Margo was his mate as well.

And that meant…

Eva felt like she was bubbling, and she could only guess that her smile in return was foolish and fizzy. The reservations she had were washing away like bad dreams. This fascinating man, and Margo, and her. All three of them, together. It was all so *right*. "Does Margo know?"

"I don't think so? She hit me over the head with a popcorn machine and the whole night is kind of a blur."

Eva wanted to shake him by the shoulders, but she could barely reach his shoulders, let alone would she be able to budge him with the action. "You have to *tell* her! *We* have to find her and tell her! What does it *mean*?" Could she have them *both*?

Never in her life had she imagined anything so beautiful.

Bruno was smiling at her, like *she* was the beautiful thing. "Can I kiss *you* first?"

She had a choice, Eva realized with joy and relief. She wanted to, but she didn't *have* to. She put her napkin carefully to the side and stood. Bruno shoved back his chair, forgetting about his own napkin, and stood to scoop her up into his arms and kiss her.

His kiss was nothing like Margo's. Margo's kiss was careful and cautious. Bruno's was purely to claim her.

13

MARGO

Harriet, or more specifically Tobias, had gone totally over the top in arranging the dinner between Eva and Bruno. He had reserved the entire arboretum and hired a private meal to be catered and served on location for just the two of them.

"This has been a great distraction, Yenta," Harriet said to Margo as she explained the plan. "Tobias gets to focus on setting his best friend up and I am off the hook for choosing *hors d'oeuvres* for another week. Weddings are an endless hassle. Anyway, he seems to think that Bruno is the perfect match for Eva, and I'm inclined to agree. He's delighted to set them up."

They *were* utterly ideal for each other, and the more that Margo learned about Bruno, the more it seemed like they were destined to be together. He was shy and good-hearted, like Eva, and he was strong to her slight.

Mates.

They were mates.

So Margo did the adult thing and set them on a path for happiness with each other.

It was slightly *less* adult of her to sneak into the arboretum so that she could assure herself that she hadn't screwed this up and that they really would be happy together, and she hadn't walked Eva into some kind of nefarious trap.

And it went perfectly to plan.

This was what you wanted, Margo told herself, watching Bruno lift Eva up into his arms and kiss her passionately. This was their fairy tale ending, and she could not allow herself to be jealous even though they were each getting what she wanted more than anything else in the world.

They would be happy together, happier than she could ever make either of them, and that would be enough. It had to be enough. It was all she had.

Bruno was setting Eva back onto her feet then, gazing into her eyes as she looked adoringly back. *I can do this,* Margo thought fiercely. *I can be happy for this, even if it's not my own happiness.*

Then Bruno put his nose in the air like he'd just smelled something, and his head swiveled straight to where Margo was standing in the shadows.

With no sense of smell of her own, Margo was never sure what her odor was doing. She cleaned faithfully and favored a lavender soap because people swore it was pleasant, but she was never entirely sure if she'd stepped in something foul or eaten a meal that gave her bad breath.

Bruno shouldn't be able to see her in the atmospheric gloom and underbrush, but Margo was sure that he had. Could he *smell* her?

Margo tried to melt away back into the underbrush, but the problem with arboretums was that they rustled like crumpled up plastic bags and she managed to step on a stray twig and knock over a potted plant.

What were you supposed to do when you were caught spying on the couple you'd just set up? Wave sheepishly?

Margo didn't have a better idea, so she gave the barest little tip of her chin in acknowledgement, then turned to go and leave them in peace.

"Margo!" Eva's call was soft and sylvan, and Margo glanced back to find that the woman had left Bruno and was running, fleet-footed and silent, straight for Margo through the trees.

This was not according to plan. This was nowhere near the plan. She should go, but she was too slow to evade Eva's hummingbird dart, and before she knew it, Eva was flinging herself up into her arms and Margo had to catch her out of reflex.

"Darling Margo!" Eva said in ecstasy, covering Margo's faces in little butterfly kisses. Was this her way of thanking Margo? Margo cradled her close, but didn't dare do more until Bruno crashed his way through the plants to catch them both up into his arms with a roar of laughter.

"What are you doing?" Margo demanded. Eva's lithe body was pressed between them, all curves and crushed black velvet.

"We're *both* his mates!" Eva cried. She had her arms around Margo's neck, and her legs wrapped around Margo's waist, and Bruno's arms were around them both. For a moment, Margo thought he might foolishly try to lift them together, but he only danced a little in place and laid a demanding kiss on Margo's lips over Eva's shoulder.

She really hoped she didn't have bad breath, but only for a brief moment before she had no breath at all.

14

BRUNO

Bruno unlocked the door to his apartment, feeling uncomfortably like there were butterflies in his stomach. He'd told Frank that the destruction was caused by vandals, but begged him to keep it quiet. Frank had guessed he was embarrassed that he'd gotten knocked out and Bruno let him think that because he didn't know how to explain having two mates.

He spent the next two weeks searching for both women in vain, with nothing to go on but the name *Eva*. He didn't want to involve police or get them in inadvertent trouble, and his efforts to get Tobias involved were hampered by his reluctance to explain two mates to him, knowing he would only make dirty jokes to make Bruno squirm. But Tobias had come through.

"Admit that I'm a genius!" the gnome said in triumph. "I found your mystery *Eva* woman and got you a date with her."

Bruno thought he could be happy with just Eva, but then Margo had crashed the meal, and he thought he understood what ecstasy could be.

Now, they were both coming home with him, and he had no idea what to do next.

Hug! his cave bear commanded. *Now!*

We can't just…hug them, Bruno protested.

Why not?

Bruno wasn't honestly sure. Shouldn't he do some wooing first, set the mood, warm things up?

Hug! his cave bear insisted.

Margo and Eva came in quietly when he opened the door for them, gazing around at his messy, pedestrian entryway. It was untidily hung with winter coats and cluttered with a broom that Bruno hadn't put away, an umbrella leftover from a season that needed it, and a pair of skis that Tobias had pressed upon him as a Christmas gift.

They all took off their boots, shaking snow onto the mat. Eva's boots were tiny compared to Bruno and Margo's; she could have slipped both of hers into any one of theirs.

It was an unimpressive home, Bruno thought in despair as he took their coats. He should have a massive and fashionable penthouse like Tobias or Frank to show them, decorated with exquisite artwork and carpeted in silk. He got so nervous that he knocked over the skis and had to juggle them back upright, bumping a painting on the wall off-kilter.

This is better than hugging?

"Do you want some refreshment?" Bruno offered. "Is it too late for coffee?" Should he find something stronger?

"We should discuss our terms," Margo said stiffly.

"Terms of coffee?" Bruno said, bewildered.

Eva gave a stifled little giggle.

How had everything gotten so awkward?

It was easier when they were kissing. But Bruno was

pretty sure that making love to them in the arboretum was against the rules of whatever strings Tobias had pulled to get them set up for dinner there, so he'd invited them here, and everything had gotten stilted on the drive over.

"This," Margo said, gesturing vaguely at all of them. "We should have ground rules. Establish boundaries. I could be the jealous type. You might have expectations I should know about."

"Such as, do we like butt stuff?" Eva asked it innocently, but her eyes were dancing.

Margo and Bruno both gave nearly identical shouts of laughter and Bruno felt his anxiety melt into amusement. It was so unexpected of Eva, and so perfect.

Margo sobered first. "I was thinking more like, do we always wait for all of us to be together, or are we allowed solo liaisons, and is it an open relationship, or do we have a custody schedule? What about kids? Living arrangements? But now I'm kind of dying to know if you do like *butt stuff,* and what, exactly, that entails."

"Oh wait," Bruno said. "Are we actually going to talk about *butt stuff?* I don't know if I can do that in a room with ladies."

"That presumes we are ladies," Margo said. "Eva may be, but I assure you I am not."

"I'm the one who brought up *butt stuff,*" Eva reminded them.

"Perhaps Bruno is the only lady present, then," Margo said, completely deadpan. "But this doesn't answer my questions, and I do think it's important to be transparent."

"I want to try *everything,*" Eva said frankly. "Everything with you." She turned from Margo to Bruno. "With you *both.*"

It would be easy to underestimate either of them, Bruno thought. Eva was so small and naive looking, and

Margo was so grim and stone-faced. He could understand why their intellect might be overlooked.

"Do we *need* a contract?" he felt comfortable enough to tease Margo.

"I like contracts," she said. "They prevent misunderstanding later. But…I think it is enough to speak your mind, to have truth and trust between us."

Yes.

Bruno's cave bear was utterly delighted and Bruno echoed him out loud. "Yes."

"Yes to a contract?" Margo said shrewdly.

"Yes to you," Bruno clarified. "Yes to you both. I don't care how we make love or what papers you want signed. I can respect you enough not to bind you to me exclusively if that was what you wished, though I would be painfully jealous if you shopped elsewhere, and I will devote my life to the two of you forever if you let me. A dozen kids or none, I'd live in a cardboard box with you or give you any space you asked for." Bruno was no poet, but he thought he'd done a pretty good job of putting those words together.

His mates both inhaled, and he could read the joy in their eyes and feel it singing in his soul.

"I do not want anything outside of this," Margo growled. She was so like his bear: strong and straightforward.

"Nor do I," Eva whispered. She was so like him: quiet, sensitive, and intense.

"I promise you this," Bruno said, digging deep past his cave bear's primal urge to take them now and make his claim a contract of flesh. "You are my soulmates. I will live my life for your pleasure and purpose. I will support and adore you. I am yours. Completely. That is my compact with you."

Eva had gone still, but Margo was taking her shirt off over her head, and was stalking towards Bruno decisively. She was gloriously curvy, her breasts cupped in a support garment that deserved more letters than B-R-A.

Bruno met her with a possessive kiss and helped her strip his own shirt off as their proximity and press of lips allowed. His cock, which had been at attention since he'd first seen Eva waiting at the table for him, was fully erect now, and Margo was the perfect height to tease him and grind her hips against him. Their hunger only heightened, they turned in unison to Eva.

To Bruno's dismay, her face was shuttered. Margo picked up on her hesitation at the same time. "We can wait, or…?"

Eva shook her head, blonde curls bouncing. "No, no, I don't ever want to wait. I just…"

Bruno waited with all the patience he could dredge up for her to continue.

"Eva?" he finally asked, when she seemed incapable of continuing.

She closed her eyes and seemed to gather herself. "I'll *show* you," she said, lifting her hands to the buttons of her shirt. She unbuttoned it gradually and slipped it from her shoulders. Margo gave a little noise of appreciation as her slight curves were revealed, barely encased in a thin white bra and if Bruno hadn't already been fully aroused, nothing could have stopped him then. Margo was close enough to his side that he could feel the warmth off of her, and it was like knowing a multi-course meal was waiting for him.

Eva reached behind herself and slipped the bra off, then turned so that her bare back was to them.

There were two jagged, angry scars from the outside of

each shoulder blade to her waist. They looked fresh, painful and red, barely past scabs.

Beside him, Margo gave a gasp of horror, and Bruno remembered how he had pulled Eva close, not knowing she was so injured. Had he hurt her when they kissed?

Squooshes? his cave bear said in consternation.

"Who did this to you?" Margo snarled.

15

EVA

*E*va had known this moment was inevitable.

She would have to reveal her shame to them at some point, and Margo's words of *truth and trust* rang in her head.

"I will make them pay," Bruno growled, following Margo's outraged exclamation, and Eva wanted to weep a little at their anger and protectiveness.

Then Margo's fingers were at her shoulder, tracing down the hateful, raw scars. "Who did this?" she repeated. Eva couldn't understand how her fingers could be so gentle when her voice was so hard.

Bruno's hand was on her opposite shoulder, though he didn't offer to touch the wounds.

"Tell me," he commanded. "Us," he corrected himself immediately. "Tell us."

Had she ruined their moment, spoiled the blooming joy? But she knew the expectations of their retreat to Bruno's apartment, and she knew that she wouldn't be able to satisfy their bond without exposing her back and all of the questions it would raise.

"I did this," she said, so quietly that she feared they wouldn't hear her. "To escape the Queen of Faery."

She needn't have worried. Shifters had keen hearing, and so, apparently, did half-trolls.

"The Queen of Faery?" Margo asked. "You were her prisoner?"

"Let me kill her for you," Bruno suggested.

"Let *me* kill her for you," Margo countered.

Eva hadn't expected their first fight to be over who got to kill someone for her, but it surprised a wry chuckle from her lips before she turned to look bravely up at both of them. "It isn't a pretty story," she cautioned them, "and I am not the hero of the tale."

"Nothing you reveal could change how I feel for you," Margo said swiftly. "Your past is in the past."

Bruno growled in agreement.

Eva drew a deep breath, taking courage from the strength and the warmth of her mates beside her. "I was the Queen of Faery's courtesan. Her favorite, for a while. I was her dressmaker, and her lover. But she was…very jealous."

"You don't have to talk about it if you don't want to," Margo growled. "But we won't love you any less, no matter what happened."

"You're *safe* here," Bruno added.

Eva looked from one of them to the other. She trusted them, and she wanted them to know the truth.

"I was flattered by her attention, and proud of my talent with fashion. I was happy for her advances, and went willingly to her bed. But sh-she was not satisfied with my affection and my obedience. She wanted *all* of me, and she enspelled me. I didn't realize at first, because it was slow and insidious, but she forced me to love her, to adore *only* her, to see *only* her. I couldn't think without thinking of her, couldn't breathe without wanting her air. I don't think she *meant* to hurt me, but it crushed me, crushed the life and soul out of me. I couldn't create; there was no room for beauty that wasn't hers, and I made dresses that were uglier and uglier without meaning to."

Eva spread her fingers and looked at them. "I thought it was a flaw in my magic, that I was not worthy, and in a fit of failure when she was away and I could not bear it, I tore my wings from my back and lost the part of me that was Faery. Destroying my own magic broke her spell. I s-saw for the first time what she'd done to me, and I fled Faery."

Eva could still feel the fiery pain of it, wrenching at her wings, scratching and clawing as if there were stitches holding them to her shoulders that she could cut away with her nails.

She still felt the clarity that flooded in after: the awful, suffocating way she'd been treated, the terrible one-sidedness of their relationship, and the artful manipulation of a woman she'd admired…and trusted. Worst of all was the emptiness that remained.

"I had nowhere to go. I had no contacts in the human world, and was slow to learn how it worked. I was in terrible debt by the time that Harriet found me."

Bruno made an understanding noise. "That's why you broke into Wilson Kinetics."

"A man named Antonio contacted me and said that he would clear my ledger if I got him the information about Frank's next sculpture. He gave me the access information and told me when to go."

"Harriet would have paid off your debt," Margo reminded her.

Eva shook her head. "She'd already done so much for me. I…even thought about stealing it. But I couldn't. This seemed like a simpler option. One job, and I'd be done. I'd be…free. I didn't want to hurt anyone. I'm so stupid…so weak…"

Her mates surrounded her, murmuring reassurance into her ear that she wasn't stupid or weak or wrong, that they forgave everything and blamed her for no part of her torment.

She wasn't sure how Margo and Bruno had gotten so close on the couch, or how she had come to be perched halfway across each of their laps, drinking in the warmth and closeness of them. Bruno's big, bare arms seemed made for stroking, and Margo's soft breasts, spilling over her rigid support garment, were begging for Eva's attention. She wouldn't have to move more than the tiniest amount to coax kisses from either of them and there was a hand resting on each of her knees.

"You aren't…worried?" she murmured. "The Faery Queen might still be looking for me."

Kisses were her answer, in her hair and on her neck, each of their hands tugging at her knees. She spread her legs and felt their fingers tighten in an unconscious reaction. She wanted them to be wild and rough with her, and she wanted their gentleness and affection, all at once. How could they be so many things at the same time?

Margo's hand was slipping up the inside of her thigh, Bruno's hand was caressing a bare breast. "The Queen of Faery couldn't keep me from you," he growled near her ear.

"She'd be welcome to try," Margo breathed on her other side. "Trolls have no allegiance to royalty and no fear of the Fae."

Eva wanted to warn them against too much confidence, to keep them from being foolishly proud of their considerable strength, but she wanted their kisses much more than their caution. She had won her freedom from the Queen of Faery, and she was with her mates in Bruno's den.

The biggest problem now was clothing, and too much of it. Eva was still wearing her pants, and Margo was still wearing her incredible tailored brassiere. Eva slipped a hand around Margo to tease out the clasps, pausing to appreciate the craftsmanship of the garment. "Who made this?" she asked breathlessly, blindly releasing the restraints.

"There's a guy off Jackson Street that does custom work. Trolls—even half-trolls—have rather particular clothing requirements. It's hellishly expensive, but worth every soul I've sold for it."

"Have you really sold souls?" Eva asked in astonishment.

"No, not really," Margo said swiftly. "It's a figure of speech." But then Eva finally worked out the last hook and the garment fell away.

Bruno gave a growl and reached across Eva for a freed breast like he couldn't help it.

Maybe he couldn't. Certainly Eva was as enraptured, and for a moment, they quarreled good-naturedly over who would caress what.

"We're all…wearing a bit…too much…still…" Margo gasped.

"I'm not sure how I'm even fitting in these pants," Bruno agreed.

That led to stripping his pants off, and Margo and Eva took gleeful turns teasing and tormenting him. Margo took his cock into her mouth, deeper with each stroke and Eva watched Bruno's hands claw into the couch cushions on either side of him.

Then they both turned their attention to Eva and were

stripping off first her pants and then, slowly, as she stood on the couch, her panties, touching her and worshiping her as they slipped them off of her.

Margo's pants went considerably faster, and somehow Eva was unsurprised to find that she was fastidiously trimmed and shaped around the warm mouth of her pussy. Bruno pushed her back onto the couch and Eva wormed her way between them to kiss Margo's glorious breasts and take each of her hard nipples in her mouth, one after another.

She felt rather than saw Bruno mount behind them, and felt his cock brush her thighs, teasing her own mound mercilessly. She made soft noises of need and ground down against Margo. Someone was kissing her ear, both of them, maybe, but all the touches seemed to blur together into one tantalizing haze of pleasure.

Margo was tight and wet around her fingers, and she tensed beneath Eva and gave a growl of release and desire just as Bruno drove into Eva and Eva had a moment of sheer joy, giving and taking delight in equal measure.

16

MARGO

The night went by in a blur of love-making and confession, telling tales of childhood and divulging dreams. They talked about where they might live, what the future could hold, how many children they wanted, what their favorite foods and flowers were. They conversed naturally, comfortable and cozy in Bruno's giant bed, until they feel asleep almost in unison.

Margo came awake first, and she could feel the warmth of Eva in her arms, and the tickle of her hair on her face. Behind her, Bruno tucked them both close. It was sticky in the space where they met, and Margo longed for the smell of her mates. She could only guess at Eva's delicate perfume and Bruno's musk. The scent of sex must be so wonderful and rich, the way it was written in books, but the descriptions always assumed a certain amount of base understanding. Roses and incense and cedar. It begged the question of what *she* smelled like, and whether it was pleasant.

She had never cared to be pleasant before.

She wanted to be efficient, logical, strong, and essentially useful. She knew she could never be less than monstrous, and strove to make up for it with functionality.

But now she wished with all of her heart to be the kind of person that these two, one that she had craved for so long, the other that had swept her off of her considerable feet with a single glance, would *desire* to be with.

Not because she was bound by destiny or magic, but because they found in her the kind of joy she found in them.

Intoxicating, wild, wonderful joy, like she'd never imagined possible. Bruno's strong arms. Eva's soft lips. She wanted to be here, forever, in this perfect moment of comfort and release.

But doubts crept in as the moment of passion ebbed into exhaustion. Bruno and Eva had so much to recommend them. Her fae beauty and gentleness. His strength and ruggedness and handsome face. But what was Margo in this union?

Was she a third wheel?

Eva was still and limp in her arms, and Bruno's breath was steady and nearly a snore.

Margo extracted herself carefully. Without her between them, Bruno and Eva sighed into each other without truly waking.

She padded into the attached bathroom and stared at her reflection in the mirror. Bruno's house was built to his height, and she could see herself clearly, without having to hunch down like she did in her own house.

I am a monster, she thought, but it was with less conviction than before. Did Bruno and Eva truly see something there that they could love? The idea filled Margo with hope and a warm sense of belonging.

She went back to the bedroom door and gazed in,

smiling tenderly. Kind, precious Eva and strong, sexy Bruno. They were *hers*.

Margo was ready to turn back to the bathroom and see if Bruno's monstrous shower was as luxurious as it looked when there was a sudden crackle to the air, like the shift in pressure before a thunderstorm. The hair at the back of her neck and her arms suddenly rose. It wasn't a sound or a light, at first, though Margo felt as if her vision was going black. She blinked, and Eva was gone, Bruno's arm and the blanket over them collapsing.

17

BRUNO

*B*runo came awake at Margo's furious cry, and clutched at suddenly empty space where Eva had been.

Even before he opened his eyes, he knew in his gut that something was wrong, and his cave bear was roaring in wordless outrage. "What happened? Where's Eva?" He pawed around in the blankets like she might be hiding there.

Margo was standing in the doorway, as naked as he was, and she was staring at the bed where Eva had been. "She was there, and then, it was like an electrical storm starting, but no flash or thunder, she was just gone. She's *gone!*"

Bruno threw every blanket and pillow off the bed, and shoved the mattress off the frame before he was convinced. Eva had truly vanished.

"The Queen of Faery?" Margo said quietly when she caught his eyes.

Bruno had already been thinking exactly that. "I will destroy her," he growled, stalking for the door.

"Clothes," Margo said. "We should wear clothes to storm Faery."

Bruno would have charged out naked, but Margo was clearly the sensible one in this whole unexpected relationship. They both dressed, and brainstormed.

"Tobias is a gnome," Bruno said. "He has underworld connections, which supposedly attach to Faery in some form. I'll call him."

Bruno found his phone under the heap of blankets. "Tobias. I need to get to Faery. The Queen kidnapped my mate. One of my mates. I have two. It's a really long story."

There was silence at the other end of the line, and then Tobias said, "Is this Bruno? The date went so well that you went home with two mates? How'd you manage that? *Ouch, I wasn't suggesting that I could do that, too, my love. You are the only owl for me. It's Bruno. He's in trouble. Something about Faery. No, it's not a euphemism. Probably.* Bruno, is it a euphemism for something? Did you actually end up with *two mates*?"

"It's not a euphemism. Two mates. The Queen took Eva. They have some *history*. Eva was her prisoner. I have to get her back. Can you get me there?"

Bruno had to explain it again, slower, twice, before Tobias truly believed that it wasn't some kind of prank or joke.

The gnome sighed. "I can get access to the underworld, but that won't get you through to Faery. There's a gate there, but gnomes don't have access to cross it without an explicit invitation."

"I can do it."

Margo had been quiet throughout their conversation, but Bruno did not assume for a moment that she wasn't listening in, thinking and worrying just as much as he was.

"How?" he asked.

"How what?" Tobias wanted to know.

"Hang on." Bruno missed the kind of phone where he could cover the receiver. He wasn't even sure where the receiver *was* on his cellphone. He smothered the whole thing in his hand.

"It is a common misconception that trolls guard bridges," Margo said gruffly. "But actually, trolls *are* bridges. Show me the gate, and I can get through it."

Bruno wished that he had the margin to explain how impressive that was. Margo was a whole lot of woman, and he would have been in awe of her even if she wasn't his mate.

She hugs well, his cave bear agreed, his priorities clearly in one place.

"Who's that?" Tobias wanted to know as Bruno uncovered the phone. "The other perp who trashed Frank's office? The one you said fell on you in the tub? She's the one who is your mate, too? Bruno, you *dog!*"

Bruno could only shrug and look adoringly at his mate. She was absolutely wondrous in every way.

18

EVA

*E*va knew before her eyes opened that she was back in Faery, and her heart had further to fall than ever.

Why had she let herself hope for happiness? She'd known that this would happen, that the Queen was jealous and petty and would want her back the *instant* she found joy.

For a brief moment, the memory of that bliss bolstered her again. Margo. Sweet, strong Margo, who had always loved her and never spoken of it. Bruno. Growly, charismatic Bruno who stole her heart and set her on fire with his first glance.

Her *mates.*

They loved her.

"I know you are awake."

The Queen's voice made the scars on Eva's back twitch in pain.

"My *Queen,*" she said, opening her eyes and sitting up. Faery was as bright as ever, the summer day like a punch in the face after the cozy winter of home. Wisteria in rainbow hues hung from the open rafters, and glistening birds the size of thumbnails darted in and out of the room.

Eva was unsurprised to find a cuff on her ankle, linked to a fine golden chain. The Queen held the other end of it, toying with it and swinging the end in a mesmerizing arc.

Eva was not the slightest bit enthralled, she was amazed to find. She had been afraid that she would fall at the Queen's feet at the first sight of her, begging her to allow Eva to return and restore her place at her side, but she felt only annoyed.

"Your magic is back," the Queen observed, stringing the fine chain between her fingers. "Or some small portion of it, at least."

Eva could not keep herself from reaching back, hoping and fearing and craving the feel of her wings again. Only scarred skin met her fingers.

Faery magic was fickle and variable, sometimes a sweeping power, sometimes a specific gift or talent, and sometimes, like now, a tiny spark that Eva recognized beneath her breastbone. It was the faintest echo of what she'd had before. She might be able to spin a basic illusion, maybe secure a few stitches in physical cloth. She could certainly not fly, or fight her way free of the delicate chain at her ankle.

"Eva…darling…"

The Queen's voice was thick with her own great magic, and Eva could feel it coiling around her, grasping and caressing…and finding no purchase.

They blinked at each other and Eva saw something in the Queen's eyes that she'd never seen there before: uncertainty.

Eva didn't have to reach for her, didn't have to worship her. She looked into those gem-green eyes and didn't feel adoring despair, only pity. The Queen didn't know what love really was, only devotion, and she didn't know how to have that without coercion. "I'm so sorry," she blurted.

"For leaving me? For breaking my heart and cleaving a hole in Faery itself?"

Eva's sympathy strained. "Don't be dramatic," she said impatiently. "I didn't do any of those things."

It was the second time that she'd surprised the Queen, and no less startling.

"No matter," the Queen said proudly. "You are back where you belong now, and I will not be so careless with you this time."

Eva felt her heart sink. "I-I do not want to stay here. I want to go back to—" *my mates*, she wanted to say, but she hesitated at the last moment. Would she put Margo and Bruno in peril if she pointed the Queen's ire at them?

"The human world?" the Queen guessed in disgust. "You want to go back to that ugly, magicless place? They have mosquitos! And poverty!"

Eva had known poverty. She had been at its mercy and made terrible deals to escape it. She was still paying off the debts it left. But she had also known hope, and the compassion of people like Harriet.

"Their food has *calories*," the Queen added with a sniff. "You are better off here, and since your judgment cannot be trusted, I will hold you here until you see the sense of it and love me again of your own will."

"No," Eva said firmly, with all the courage she had learned.

"No?" The Queen said the word as if she was unfamiliar with it, and maybe she was. Her court was full of magic bound to her rule.

"No," Eva repeated boldly. "I will not love you again. I never did, not the way you wished I would. I was never whole with you, and I will never willingly stay with you again."

The Queen rose and bristled, her angry power causing the flowers to shrink into themselves and the birds to flee. Even the brilliant fae light seemed to dim in the face of her fury…and Eva was not afraid. The Queen's fury was like a storm breaking over stone, energy that would wash away after it had tantrumed itself out.

There was no substance to the Queen, not now that Eva knew what true love and true loyalty was. "You cannot keep me," she said softly. "I am not yours."

"If you are not mine, you will certainly not be anyone else's," the Queen snapped, and she swirled and vanished with the scent of honey and burnt sugar.

The chain at Eva's ankle shimmered with no end, but the shackle remained. Eva settled back on the bed as the flowers shyly opened again in the wake of the Queen's departure, and a few brave birds flitted in to taste them.

The magic might hold her here, but it could never touch her heart again.

19

BRUNO

"Well, this is as far as I can get you," Tobias said, swinging the beam of his flashlight over the end of the tunnel.

The passage they stood in was short, far too short for Bruno to comfortably stand. Bruno and Margo were both half-crouched, staring at the door they'd been led to.

Bruno wasn't sure what he'd expected the gates of Faery to look like. Gold filigree, maybe, or made of flowers. It ought to be magical, Bruno thought, and magical ought to look *fancy*.

This was not fancy.

The door had rusted iron bands patterned over graying wood. There were silhouettes of animals carved all over it. Was it supposed to imply a zoo?

It was definitely the door of someone who wanted to keep people out, not invite them in.

Tobias tapped his flashlight on one of the iron bars, but there was no answer. "Really not sure what you'll do from here. This thing never opens."

"It will open for me," Margo said firmly. "Please stand back."

Tobias very sensibly scooted back behind Bruno.

But when Bruno expected her to charge forward and try to take it on with her shoulder, Margo merely took her own flashlight and frowned at the door, inspecting every edge and hinge and latch and grain of wood.

"Is she looking for a weak spot?" Tobias asked.

"Yes," Margo said shortly. "What would you say this door looks like?"

"A prison door?" Bruno said.

"A trunk?" Tobias suggested.

Margo nodded. "And what has a trunk?" It wasn't a question. She put her hand over the image of an elephant, said loudly, "Open!"

To everyone's surprise except Margo's, it did.

Tobias whistled as the door cracked open. The tunnel continued beyond it, to a far-off glimpse of daylight at the end. "Nice trick," he said.

"It will be different for the next person," Margo cautioned. "Faery doors always are."

"When did you become an expert on Faery?" Tobias asked.

"Last night," Margo said with a sideways glance. "The Faery Code is available online."

The door shut behind them with a clang of finality.

"How did you know what to do with the door?" Bruno asked, as he crouched to clear the doorframe, following Margo through. The tunnel was, if anything, even lower past the door.

"Gates and bridges always whisper their secrets," Margo said.

"Magic?"

"Not like spells or witchcraft," Margo was quick to explain, glancing back over her shoulder at Bruno. "It's more like shifter strength. A natural part of being a troll."

"Like my keen sense of smell," Bruno agreed.

"I don't have a sense of smell," Margo said, and Bruno thought she sounded regretful. "Maybe this is what I have instead."

"How curious," Bruno said. He worried that it didn't sound as admiring as he felt, but it was hard to converse to Margo's back end, however nice it was, when they were both half-bent over and scuttling down a damp tunnel like lost crabs.

Hug her, his cave bear advised unhelpfully.

That's your solution for everything. "What else should I know about Faery?"

"Don't say *thank you*," Margo cautioned. "Faery takes debts very seriously and *thank you* can imply a favor owed. You don't want a faery owing you a favor."

"What about *please*?"

"*Please* is perfectly safe."

The floor of the tunnel crunched like gravel underfoot and Bruno tried not to imagine that it was the bones of trespassers.

"What's our plan of attack once we get there?" Bruno asked. Margo was so astonishingly capable, he might be intimidated if he wasn't so enraptured with her.

"There's no way to take Eva by force," Margo cautioned. "Faery magic isn't about strength, and we have no power here anyway. I will have to open a challenge for her hand."

"Shouldn't that be me?" Bruno wanted to know. Margo was gorgeously strong and fierce, but it was hard to top a cave bear in battle or brute strength.

"Do you trust me?" Margo stopped so abruptly that Bruno ran into her from behind.

Hug! his cave bear insisted, and Bruno let himself indulge. "I trust you," he said faithfully.

It was not the most graceful hug, with both of them stooped beneath the short stone ceiling, but he felt Margo relax gratefully into him. "Then let me challenge."

As they walked, she told him more. "Under current code, challenges in Faery are very peculiar. A challenge may be brought against anyone, once. The challenged chooses the battlefield, the challenger chooses the weapons."

It was certainly *challenging* to track all of the parties, Bruno thought. "What about me?"

"If I fail, you can challenge again, your way, and you have three days to do it. Things in threes are important to them, like the three impossible tasks and the three nights spent at a lover's door that you hear in stories."

"Maybe it's lucky that there are three of us," Bruno suggested. He was sure they would be victorious. They would save Eva and be home before dinner. "Do I have to worry about eating faery food?" he asked, because the reminder of dinner made his stomach complain audibly.

"If they offer it, it must be served without strings," Margo assured him. "That's a change in the most recent version of the Code."

"Did you read the whole thing?"

"It was only two hundred pages. And some of it was appendixes. I skimmed those."

The tunnel finally rose and opened out into a meadow of rainbow grass that reflected a brilliant white-gold sky. Bruno blinked, trying to adjust his eyes to the sudden brightness, and found himself focusing on the tip of a spear. A knight clad in oddly-jointed armor towered above him until Bruno remembered that he could stand upright again, and then he was eye-to-eye with an eye-slit in a helmet that showed no actual eyes.

"Take us to your leader," Margo said in a perfect deadpan.

And it did.

20

MARGO

Faery wasn't quite what Margo was expecting.

Besides being very bright and rather technicolor, it also seemed rather…flimsy.

It was like walking through a movie set; everything looked very grand and impressive from one angle, but when she stepped to the side, it was suddenly flat, and metaphorically propped up with wooden braces from behind.

"It's all illusions," Bruno said, when the flower he plucked and tried to give to Margo turned into little dancing motes of light that floated away.

Margo tried to catch the little particles before they escaped, and they slipped through her fingers with the sound of giggles.

Their travel was discontinuous. A valley would stretch out before them for miles, but it could be simply crossed with a few firm strides. Jagged peaks of ice rose before them, but melted away into lace arches and bowers of flowers.

Even with their long legs, Margo and Bruno had to

half-jog to keep up with the clanking empty armor, and it wasn't long until they were entering a forest grotto hung in chiming silver bells and riotous green vines. Figures were milling in the sweet-shadowed underbrush, eclectic and as varied as the shifting landscapes. Most of them had wings, but they were all sorts of wings; leathery batwings, feathered like a bird, or translucent like an insect. Some of them seemed made entirely of light and Margo thought one was simply vibrating air. They came in all sizes, some with knees at eye-level and some barely a handspan tall.

"Eva!"

Margo had been watching her feet, because there were tiny fairies at the edges of the lawn that she didn't wish to step on, and she looked up to see Eva sitting at the feet of the Queen of Faery on a dais, dressed in a gossamer tunic that didn't suit her at all.

Relief flooded her, because Eva looked whole and hale, then rage rose up in her like a storm. There was a golden shackle on one slim ankle, and a fine chain that ran to the Queen's wrist.

She grabbed for Bruno's arm before the cave bear shifter could surge forward and try to take Eva by force, recognizing the delicate magic and the even more delicate balance of power.

"We're in her court," she hissed. "Be careful what you *say*."

"Welcome!" the Queen called, as they stepped into the dancing forest shadows. "Tell me, mortals, how did you find your way to Faery without an invitation?"

Margo shushed Bruno with a hand on his arm. "Your majesty, we came in search of our mate." It wasn't exactly an answer to her question, but she didn't want to volunteer more than she had to.

This invited a murmur of speculation from their diverse audience.

"Hmm," the Queen said, stroking the chain that she held loosely in her hands. "And you come to challenge my champion for her?"

"You choose the place, I choose our weapons," Margo confirmed, casting her eye over the warriors who flanked the Queen. There was an armored centaur, a scaled lizard in spiked leather, and a gargoyle-like man made of stone muscle who wore nothing at all.

The Queen's confidence was unsettling. "Indeed."

Margo knew her limits. Her fighting prowess was considerable, but only because of her size and strength. These were each more than a fair match for her and probably had better training in skirmish. She had a chance. But not a good one.

"I agree," Margo said, ignoring Bruno's growl beside her. "Don't interfere," she whispered aside. "It has to play out according to the *rules*." His hand in hers tightened, but he didn't stop her.

The Queen made a show of selecting her champion, walking slowly down her line, stroking muscles and drawing her finger along the sharp edges of their weapons. Eva's chain dangled beside her, expanding as the distance between them grew. Eva clung to the side of the throne but made no move to try to approach them. Her eyes were little gems of hope and Margo prayed that she would not let her mate down with this desperate gamble.

The Queen finally snapped her fingers to the gargoyle, who lumbered forward and bowed to her. He had stone wings at his back that looked functional, and carved fur that kept his naked lower half company-respectable. His beast-like face was framed in large ears and wicked claws flexed on his dexterous hands. "I will champion you," he hissed in a guttural voice.

"See that you do," she said, turning back to Margo. "This place will serve as a battlefield. Choose your weapon." She gestured to a rack of sharp spears and curved swords.

"I choose riddles," Margo said firmly.

There was silence in the court and all of the amusement faded from the Queen's face. "What do you mean?"

Margo picked her words with extraordinary care. "I choose a battle of *cleverness.* Faery prides itself on playing fair and swears by the Code. Prove it."

"You want to make it a battle of *wits*? With *me*?"

"Not you, your majesty. Your *champion.*"

The audience murmured in interest. The gargoyle had clearly been chosen for his physical prowess, and Margo's brute strength had been her most obvious bid for championship. In a battle of might, either of one of them might prevail.

"And who do you suggest will mediate this duel of *riddles*?" The Queen's disgust was as clear as her doubt of Margo's intelligence.

Margo had already considered this question. "I propose a jury of peers. Let a panel of your subjects choose the winner."

"Do you believe you would receive impartiality from people who call *me* their queen?"

"Will you command it from them?" Margo countered.

The court was absolutely silent and for a moment, Margo feared that her gambit would fail before it began.

"One more thing," Margo said. "No magical influence. No spells or enchantments or illusions. Make it a *fair* battle."

There was a flicker in the Queen's eyes, just a hint of

something behind her icy gaze. Margo wouldn't have recognized it if she didn't know her own stony face so well. Was she angry that Margo had imposed a handicap…or did she *regret* her treatment of Eva?

"No magical influence," the Queen agreed quietly. She loftily added, "I won't need it."

"Wait!" the gargoyle growled, chilling Margo's swell of hope. "No riddles requiring obscure human knowledge. It should be an honest contest."

"An honest match," Margo agreed. "The committee shall determine if a riddle is unfair."

"I look forward to a good challenge," the gargoyle said, his stone face curving up into a smile.

Margo didn't like the glint in his eyes, and she found herself wondering if she'd just made a terrible mistake.

21

EVA

*E*va wished she could warn Margo about the flaw in her plan, or speak to her mates at all, but the chain at her ankle silenced her lips as well as keeping her clasped at the Queen's side. She could only fume on the inside, and despair. It was probably just as well. She was likely to blubber. They had come to save her, and Eva was full of embarrassing tender feelings.

"It will take some time to put together this jury," the Queen said.

"The Code allows three days to prepare for any duel," Margo said, nodding. "Either contestant can request it."

"You know our Faery Code?" the Queen said suspiciously.

"It's online," Margo said briefly. "Filed at knowyourcodes.org with the legal edicts of seven hundred states and countries. I brushed up after you *kidnapped my mate.*"

"I don't need three days." The Queen made a dismissive gesture. "We can convene in an hour."

"I do not object to this," Margo said, with equal coolness.

Eva felt her heart soften. Margo was so clever and capable, and so brave to come to try to save her. How could she not love the woman? Bruno was exciting and sexy, and Margo was comfortable and compelling, and together they were the best mates anyone might ask for.

The Queen reached over and stroked Eva's short hair, interrupting her swell of joy and hope. Eva shook her head in annoyance and the Queen took her hand back rather quickly, probably not happy with the show of defiance.

Well, Eva was done with being a good little pet, and she didn't care who saw it. She wasn't afraid anymore, and she wasn't enamored with the Queen and never would be again.

"Go prepare them for the trial," the Queen snapped. "Garb them in clothing appropriate for proceedings and offer them refreshment." She rose and started forming the riddle committee.

Each of the fae that the Queen selected solemnly swore to cast their vote fairly, and she spun them a marble bench and built a courtyard of stone, lace, and vines. They were a motley bunch, some slight fairies with glittering wings, some wild ones with horns and lichen hair, a few with animal halves, and two chuckling giants. This was the greatest spectacle in memory: a troll from the human world, companioned by a cave bear, taking on Faery's stone champion in a battle of wits for the rescue of the Queen's favorite lost toy.

The Queen was sometimes like a child, wanting what she couldn't have, but she was clever and canny, and she had not kept her throne by being reckless or foolish. Her champion was not the brainless brawn that Margo would be expecting, and her fight would be no less fraught for being of words and not swords.

When they reconvened, Margo and Bruno had been

given faery robes in gold and red. The gargoyle and the Queen were garbed in silver and green. Eva distracted herself by analyzing the designs and finding fault in the flow of the fabric. She would never put Margo in such bold designs; Margo was subtle and beautiful in a way that wasn't so showy. And why disguise Bruno's fine physique with such unnecessary flounce? He'd be better served in something more fitted and understated. Something that flattered his shoulders.

Every magical stitch was purposeful, Eva thought, because *image* was so much a part of this game.

Margo's face was set in cool lines, but Eva could see the stress in her neck. Bruno made no effort to hide his helpless fury. He didn't like this any more than she did.

A woodling banged a gavel from the edge of the jury's bench. "We call to order this challenge."

The Queen graciously gestured Bruno forward. "Will you introduce the challenger?"

Bruno had clearly not been expecting to speak, and he looked wildly around. "I am...ah, Bruno. Bruno Bigliotti. I name my mate, Margo Meret, as the challenger, to fight for the hand of Eva Singer. Who is also my mate. I...ah... hope you will judge objectively and...ah...have a good day?"

The jury murmured a little, and laughed. It was not kind laughter.

The Queen stepped forward in a swirl of skirts. "I am your Queen, your loving liege, the Flower of Fae. I name as my champion Gary, my most loyal and trustworthy warrior, as clever in words as he is in blades. I bid you judge *fairly*!" She blew them a kiss at the end.

Did that count as swaying the jury? Eva ground her teeth in frustration as Margo and Gary stepped forward.

"This timer shall be the limit of the riddle," the Queen

said, handing a golden hourglass to the woodling who was speaker of the jury. "A fair riddle must be given and answered in this time." She demonstrated its use and the woodling reset it several times to ensure it could be done instantaneously.

The Queen raised a hand into the air and a swarm of fuzzy bees descended onto it. When they lifted away, she had a gold coin in her hand. "We shall flip to see who goes first." She held up the coin and showed that it had two sides, a crown and a triskelion, their symbolism obvious. She handed it to a member of the jury, who tossed it gleefully into the air and let it fall to the ground. It landed triskelion up.

The Queen graciously gestured to Margo, who stepped forward and gathered it up.

"I'm sorry, do you have a name?" Margo turned to return the coin to the Queen with her brow artfully furrowed. "The rest of us have provided our true names as a part of these proceedings, but you have only supplied a *title.*"

"You surely don't believe those rumors that *names* have power over the fae and are trying to trick me into revealing it," the Queen said with a smirk, snatching the coin back.

"I am only requesting it as a courtesy," Margo said blandly. "There is no magical influence permitted, and of course we would honor that as well as expect it, but there is a subconscious advantage to being referred to solely as an honorific, and that may play into the committee's decisions without *intention.*"

Clever, Eva thought. She was reminding the Queen and the jury about the magical influence agreement, without making it a point of contention, and she was doing it in such a way that it would be rude to refuse her request.

The Queen frowned, but seemed unable to find a compelling reason not to give it.

"Katerina," she finally said.

Eva shivered, wondering if the name really did have some power even without magic. She had never known it. The woman had only ever been *the Queen*, even when barriers of pleasure were dropped.

BRUNO

*B*runo wished it was a fight of swords or fists. He understood that kind of battle. Someone got pounded until they didn't want to get up, and that was the end of it.

He wasn't sure where a battle of riddles concluded, and he didn't want to look more stupid by asking.

Margo, clever, savvy Margo, gazed at her opponent. "What is it that falls standing, but runs lying down?"

The gargoyle was silent for an inscrutable moment. "Rain," he said gravely. Bruno was not sure if he'd had to think about it, or if he was just pausing for effect. "What gets wet the more it dries?"

"A towel." Margo actually smiled slightly. "What babbles but never talks?"

"A brook," the gargoyle said without hesitation. "Until I am measured, I am not known. Yet how you miss me when I have *flown*. What am I?"

Margo was thoughtful. "Flow follows a theme of water…"

"Is that your guess?" Gary asked shrewdly.

"The answer is *time*," Margo said firmly. "But I admire you for trying to trick me!"

Bruno told his jealous cave bear that she was not actually *admiring* the gargoyle as the jury applauded and chuckled.

Hug, his cave bear muttered, and it was the rib-crushing kind of hug.

"How much dirt is in a hole that is two feet by three and one third?" Margo asked.

The gargoyle's eyes narrowed. "None; it is a hole. What is on the ground but also a hundred feet in the air?"

Margo had to think about that one, her mouth pursing before she burst out. "A hundred feet—a centipede on its back!"

The jury laughed out loud, and a giant in the back pounded the arm of his chair. Bruno thought that they were enjoying the contest, and surely Margo and Gary seemed to be. Eva, still strangely mute, was watching avidly, and Bruno longed to go to her, to pick her up and make sure that she was unharmed.

Hug, his cave bear agreed plaintively.

"What is orange and sounds like a parrot?" Margo asked.

This appeared to stump the gargoyle, at least momentarily. "You cannot riddle about obscure human world animals," he protested. "I do not know all their sounds. You'd best find another riddle before your time to ask it runs out."

Margo's face remained unchanged but Bruno caught the corner of her mouth twitching. "No additional knowledge is necessary," she said smoothly.

Gary considered that, then exclaimed in triumph, "A carrot!"

The jury applauded.

Gary appeared shaken by his own hesitation and he took almost the time on the sandglass to come up with his own riddle. "What tastes better than it smells?" he asked quickly.

Margo blinked, and Bruno remembered her confession about trolls having no sense of smell. Was this an unfair riddle? He eyed the jury, but they were watching the combatants raptly and probably didn't know about her handicap. Should he volunteer the information? Would it embarrass Margo?

Hug.

I'm pretty sure hugging her in the middle of her trial won't help anything.

"A tongue," Margo said at last.

Bruno sat back with a sigh of relief.

"Forward, I am heavy. Backwards, I am not."

Gary's stone brow furrowed as he murmured the clue over under his breath. "I am *not*… Ton!"

He gave his riddle as Bruno was still trying to work out how the answer worked (T-O-N, heavy. N-O-T, backwards!) and the cave bear missed the clue, but Margo easily answered, "A stamp."

She considered for a moment, then asked, "What starts with an E and ends with an E and only has one letter?"

"That one might have been trickier, if it hadn't followed stamp," Gary pointed out. "An envelope, of course. What word becomes shorter as you add more letters?"

"That one might have been trickier, if it hadn't followed a riddle about words," Margo retorted. "Short. What belongs to you, but everyone else uses it?"

Gary glanced behind him at the Queen, who had her mouth in a tight line. Clearly, she had expected her champion to win over Margo more quickly. "A name," he said quietly. "Or a title, perhaps."

The jury murmured over this answer for a moment and then allowed it.

Gary drew himself up. He was taller than Margo by a handspan. "I appear once a minute, twice a moment, but never in one hundred thousand years. What am I?"

Margo stewed over this one almost until the sand timer ran out. "M!" she cried, as the final sands fell.

Bruno let his breath out in a huff as the jury approved her answer.

"What is taken before you can get it?" Margo asked.

Gary opened his mouth and shut it. "Honor?" he finally guessed, as the sands of his own timer finally ran out.

"A photo," Margo answered in triumph.

"Objection!" the Queen cried. "That is obscure and human!"

"A photo is obscure?" Margo looked genuinely taken aback.

"We do not have cameras in faery. I submit that this riddle is unfair."

Gary scowled.

The jury consulted.

Bruno thought their heated discussion looked much more like a battle than Margo and Gary's competition, and it was everything he could do not to wade into the argument that ensued and knock heads together to make them see Margo's side. He caught Eva's gaze from across the makeshift courtroom and she shook her head just slightly, warning him not to.

So much was at stake. How could he leave this kind of decision to a rag-tag bunch of fae fools? His mates were his, and this was all *nonsense*. But Bruno trusted his mates, and Margo was waiting quietly. She and Gary were like stone sentries on either side of a bridge, and it wasn't long before the jury got themselves back in order.

"We rule this riddle unfair," the woodling said, looking even more like they'd just been through a tornado than they had. "We declare the winner to be the Queen's gargoyle."

"Don't I get to ask another?" Margo protested.

"You had to ask a *fair* question in the time given by the glass," the woodling said regretfully. "Those are the rules."

What does this mean? Bruno wondered in horror. If Margo lost…

"Come, troll," the Queen said imperiously. "You are mine as well, now."

A gold shackle appeared on Margo's boot at the ankle, and a strand of gold chain as fine as Eva's came to the Queen's hand.

Bruno surged to his feet with a roar that he didn't even try to hold back.

23

MARGO

It took three goblins, two shrieking dryads, and a pile of rocks in the general shape of a snowman to subdue Bruno as a cave bear. Finally, one of the giants from the jury simply sat on him, and would not let him up until Bruno had pounded the ground with a fist in defeat and shifted back to a man.

The Queen tsked disapprovingly and made the mess that Bruno had made of the jury box and courtyard vanish with the wave of her hand.

Margo herself only felt numb.

She'd lost. She'd gambled her own freedom for Eva's and *lost.*

She hadn't let herself think about the possibility while she was competing, focused on each puzzle in turn, listening for the clues and centering herself on the solution. *Was* her question unfair? *Was* it a rightful loss?

Eva rose up to her feet as Margo stumbled for the dais, dragged along by the persistent pull at her ankle. Her shackle was as delicate as Eva's, and looked out of place around her rugged boot. She should have been able to break it with a pinky, but she knew better than to try.

She sank to her knees and was in reach of Eva, who came to wrap her small arms around Margo's big frame.

"Margo," she said, as if it was very difficult. "Brave, clever Margo."

"I lost," Margo murmured. "I'm sorry, I lost."

"But you came for me," Eva said adoringly. "You both did."

"Wait a second now," Bruno said. "I get a chance to challenge, too, right?"

All the attention in the court landed on him. "You do," the Queen said, swinging the ends of the gold chains. "But you can only challenge for *one* of them."

"You'd make me *choose*?"

"Take Margo!" Eva cried. "Take Margo and go free!"

"Take Eva," Margo protested. "I'm stronger than Eva."

"Can I trade myself for the freedom of both of them?" Bruno asked, in his hopefully golden retriever fashion.

The Queen looked between them all in disgust. "I could just keep you all," she said. "*Choose*, cave bear. Choose one to challenge for, or lose them both."

Margo cleared her throat. "Well, technically…"

"Don't quote Code at me, troll," The Queen snapped. She twitched the gold chain and Margo could feel the reprimand vibrate through her boot.

With effort, Margo didn't flinch. "Bruno has three days to decide. He can take that long to make up his mind before you force it on him."

The Queen's beautiful face was considerably less beautiful as she pursed her lips. "Very well," she said at last, settling back in her chair waving her hand as if it didn't matter very much. "You may enjoy the hospitality of Faery for that time."

Margo already didn't think much of the hospitality of Faery, but she gravely nodded. "Than——" She caught herself. "Your majesty is fair."

At her feet, Eva touched the Queen's foot hopefully. "Please, may I be with them during these? Show them the wonders of your realm?" She didn't have to say that it might be her last chance with them.

The pain in Margo's chest from her failure was twisted deeper watching Eva plead with the Queen, who looked down at her confidently. "Go and be with them one last time," she said with arch graciousness. "Even if he succeeds, one of you will be mine forever after that."

24

EVA

All the beautiful places in Faery that Eva had missed were even more beautiful when she showed them to her mates.

The wish falls were crimson in this season. "Be careful," she warned. "The stones are slippery, but if you wish unwittingly, it will still come true." Scarlet water scattered over stones like wine and feathery rainbow ferns grew in fringes all around the little intermittent pools. Singing reeds whispered little songs of promise and pretend, spinning stories from fish dreams.

But more beautiful than the sight of it was the way that Margo looked around in wonder, and how Bruno breathed in deep, reveling in the chocolate scent of the afternoon fog and the cedar smell of the evening rainbows.

Eva watched them more than the marvels, drinking in the dear planes of their faces and the flicker of their expressions. How had she ever thought that Margo was stone-faced? Was it possible that she'd only known Bruno a few short days? They were so familiar and right, and they followed her fearlessly up into the tree canopies and across the rope bridges over the ravine of broken dreams.

They slept the first night in a mossy grove and Eva woke when the stars were being strung for the morning constellations, feeling a familiar tug as she opened her eyes and found herself *somewhere else*.

The Queen was no less lovely than ever, and Eva braced herself for the aching pull that never came. She was beautiful, naked except for her flower-adorned hair, but Eva knew what love was now, and had no need for empty faery splendor.

"You know your thrall has no power over me now," she reminded the Queen. "Why did you bring me back?"

"I *missed* you. I missed what we had. Did I truly never mean *anything* to you?" The Queen's expression might have been artfully pained, but Eva couldn't be sure. Even without magic, she still had the power to hurt Eva's heart.

"I never had the freedom to find out," Eva pointed out. "You were my Queen. We were never equals, even before you enchanted me."

"But you adored me before," the Queen insisted. "You made me a dress of starlight flowers and sweet grass that made the court weep."

"I loved making that dress," Eva admitted. "It was inspired, and I was the happiest person in Faery when you wore it and then when you let me take it off of you."

"Then why wouldn't you stay with me? Why couldn't you love me that much without magic?"

"What we had wasn't love," Eva told her. "I'm not sorry I left."

"The human world is ugly and uncaring," the Queen argued. "People there suffer and starve. What could it offer you that I can't?"

"Happiness," Eva said simply. "My own *whole* happiness."

"You said you were happiest making me the dress of starlight…"

"I said I was the happiest person in *Faery*. The merriment here, the parties, the glitter—it's all shallow and *fake*. All this magic, and no one ever *makes* anything. You only noticed me because I was different. I wanted to do things with my hands, not spinning illusions like everyone else. I never wanted illusions, and that's all we ever were! It's real in the human world, and it's not always pretty, but it's always real…and real is better than pretty."

"I could give you back your power," the Queen said. "You could have your wings and magic back. Keep the troll and the bear as your pets, and rule at my side."

"They aren't my pets," Eva said patiently. "They are my mates."

"How is that different?" the Queen asked, and although her voice was angry, Eva thought that the question was genuine. "Your mates. Aren't you forced to love them just as much as I ever did?"

"Not even a little," Eva said immediately. "It's a calling, not a compulsion. It's the difference between a hankering for a cupcake and an addiction to drugs. My body, my heart, my soul, they *want* them, not because of the consequences of not having them, but because I know how much better and happier I'd be *with* them."

"Cupcakes aren't healthy," the Queen pointed out. Eva observed that she seemed sulky, but she hadn't shut down the way that Eva kept expecting her to.

"Sometimes a craving is for something your body needs. Sometimes, it's an indulgence. It's always a choice. I never had a choice with you. I never knew what I actually wanted for myself."

"You *chose* to leave."

"I needed to know who I was without you in my chest forcing every heartbeat to your rhythm. I'm not sorry I did it, even though it hurt worse than anything I'd ever done in my entire life. I found out who I was without you, and I found people who loved me without strings and clauses and Codes."

"Did you love me?"

"Did you love *me*?" Eva countered. "Or did you just love having power over me? Did you ever once wonder if I was *happy?*"

The Queen vanished in a puff of glitter and a hum of angry bees, and Eva woke up cradled between Margo and Bruno, exactly where she ought to be.

25

MARGO

aery was full of wonders, but none of them was quite as wonderful as being with Margo's mates.

Margo had never seen the point of leisure, until she had mates to love and be loved by, and half the fun of being able to walk on golden clouds was holding onto their hands as she went, and swimming with them in a lake that sang instead of splashed. They laughed together, and told stories, comparing everything they loved and didn't.

They made love in steaming pools and soft beds of moss and fields of flowers, in pairs and together, as the mood struck. There was a library made of flower-bound books and Margo read poetry that made her heart feel like a chest full of caged birds.

They quarreled over who Bruno should choose, until they couldn't bear to speak of it, and forgave each other with kisses and assured him that they would love him forever no matter what he was forced to decide.

The second night was spent on a mountaintop

wreathed in stars that would come down and dance on the rocks. Bruno and Eva slept curled together on a bed of cloudmatter under downy blankets while Margo measured the unfamiliar constellations with her outstretched hands and wondered if Faery astronomers were a thing that existed.

She didn't realize that she'd fallen asleep at their feet until she was dreaming, and the Queen came to her.

"Leave me Eva of your free will and I will not make Bruno decide between you or battle to free you and risk his own freedom," the Queen promised. "You can go in peace."

Margo pinched herself, because she wanted to make sure that she was dreaming. Her skin was like velvet and pain was a weird echo of sound. She could look down and see herself, curled at Bruno and Eva's feet. She was definitely dreaming. But Margo was equally sure that this was real.

"You'd just be asking me to choose, instead of Bruno," Margo observed. "It's no less cruel."

"Do you really think I'm cruel?" the Queen asked winsomely. "I promise, I am only trying to keep what I love!"

"You don't love Eva," Margo said, and she said it with genuine pity. "Love doesn't want to control and overpower. If you loved Eva, you would let her go."

"I can sweeten the deal." At first, Margo thought that the Queen was growing, that she was flexing her power and proving her strength with supernatural size. Then Margo realized that she herself was the one changing, shrinking and compressing into herself.

The Queen had not gone so far as to make Margo slight—she still had curves of substance and strength, but she was no longer freakishly tall or broad-shouldered. There was feminine grace to her lines, her muscles softened and her shape refined. Her wrists were delicate. Margo could not help herself from reaching for her face to see if it had changed from its familiar blockish planes, and that was when she realized what else the Queen was offering her.

She was human.

Simple, normal human—and with that came a sense of smell.

"I wanted you to know what you were missing," the Queen said in her silkiest voice. "*All* the little details." She gave an imperious wave of her hand and Eva's scent overwhelmed Margo.

Margo didn't have the names for the things she smelled, only the ideas, but she was sure that it must be butterscotch and clove, with hints of licorice and fresh-cut grass, complex and sweet. She opened her mouth in awe and found that there were more variations at the back of her throat, as if she was breathing Eva herself in.

She turned in wonder to Bruno and found that she could smell him as well, a hot musky wave of metal and machines, with hints of cedar and moss.

They continued their enchanted slumber and Margo realized that her eyes were welling as she gazed down at them, reveling in this new layer of their wonderful appeal. She closed her eyes so that smell was the only sense she had, and then she shook her head.

"I don't want this," she said, and she felt the truth of it as she opened her eyes. "My mates love me just the way I am. I don't need to be delicate or human or look different. I don't need to smell them to know them."

The Queen's face went icy cold and more beautiful

than ever and she shivered in place and vanished as Margo woke to find herself tangled in Bruno's arms, with Eva curled between them.

Their scent was gone, but there were still tears on her cheeks.

BRUNO

When the third day dawned, Bruno still wasn't sure what answer he was going to give.

But he knew the answer he *wouldn't* be giving. "I can't lose either of you," he said, pulling them both close as they walked to the Queen's court, the golden chains at his mates' ankles pulling them back. "I refuse. I'll get...a Faery lawyer to handle it like a custody case or something. I'll take on two Champions at once for both of you. I'll eat the Faery Code and spit it out on the Queen."

"You have to challenge for Eva," Margo said at once. "Get her out of here. I'll be alright. I'm stronger than she is."

"Take Margo," Eva protested. "The Queen can't hurt me like she once could, and Margo doesn't know Faery like I do."

Bruno gathered them both into his arms, Eva tucking perfectly into all the places between Margo and himself. They were like the pieces of one of Frank's machines, engineered to be together in every way. "I love you both," he said simply. "I can't choose between you. It's the cruelest thing she could ask of me."

Eva chuckled, muffled between them. "She thought she could tempt me back," she observed wryly. "She came to me in my dreams and tried to offer me my heart's deepest wishes to stay with her and rule by her side."

"She came to me, too," Margo said softly, stroking Eva's short hair. "She said that if I convinced you to stay, she could make me…not a monster."

"You aren't a monster," Eva protested as Bruno growled in agreement.

"She offered to take away all the things that make me feel like a monster," Margo amended. "But I told her that I already had that, because of the way you two look at me. I don't think she understands love."

"She understands what people *think* they want," Bruno said thoughtfully.

"What did she offer you?" Margo wanted to know.

Bruno felt his ears heat and his cave bear squirm. "I don't want to say," he protested. "It's enough that I said no."

There was a sudden disruption from the fringes of the crowd and the court parted in confusion as familiar figures pressed through.

"Move it, goat-man!" Harriet's ringing voice sent a horned satyr scurrying away. "I'm on the clock to meet with my wedding quartet and you're in my way. I've got a duel to fight, do you want to make it two?"

Tobias, despite his short stature, was not at all lost in the crowd as he strode at Harriet's side and let her clear the way. "You really do *not* want to fight her," he cheerfully warned the others.

"Harriet?" Margo's voice cracked in surprise.

"Tobias?" Bruno could not quite squelch his sudden feeling of hope.

"How did you get here?" the Queen asked crossly. "Do the gates of Faery mean nothing?"

"Your gargoyle buddy sent us an invitation," Harriet said. The Queen shot Gary an outraged look, but Harriet went on. "Eva and Margo are *my* employees, and I'm not losing them to some stuffed-up royal tart when I've finally got the business going smoothly. And I need Eva to design my wedding dress. I'm not settling for some off-the-rack affair when I could have one of her pieces."

The Queen's porcelain skin went almost green. "Your human contracts have no weight here."

"Sure," Harriet said. "But I've read your precious Code. Bruno, you want to challenge for Eva and I'll challenge for Margo? Either way, really."

"You will lose *too*," the Queen hissed. "I'll just add more to my collection."

"I would challenge for either of them," Tobias said, stepping forward.

"And when *you* lose?"

"Excuse me! Sorry! Coming through!"

The path in the crowd had closed and scattered again in surprise as a second pair came hurrying up. Frank and Anita were both carrying wide trays covered in careful little towers of frothy dessert.

Anita was apologizing to everyone. "I'm so sorry we're late. The cupcakes had to cool enough to frost!"

"You brought cupcakes?" Harriet asked in disgust. "We're here for a *duel*."

"Of course!" Anita said, nearly tipping over her tray in her eagerness. "But who wants to fight when there are cupcakes? There was nothing in the Code about *not* having refreshments. Try this one, it's blueberry lemon with a sprinkle of cardamom! I invented it this morning!"

"Is there a place we could put these down?" Frank asked courteously. "I might have to fight with someone to save Tobias or Bruno, and I don't want to put them on the ground."

"Does Faery have ants?" Anita asked eagerly, gazing around. "I've never been here before."

Some of the Queen's court melted away and returned with tables that appeared to be made of rigid lace. Anita cooed over them and put her tray down, immediately pausing to fix a smudged icing job as she chattered on. "It's a *French* buttercream frosting, because I wasn't sure how hot it would be or how long they would be out. That three day clause sort of complicates things, doesn't it? The last thing I wanted to do is give everyone food poisoning! Not that I've ever poisoned anyone, I promise."

"Sugar poisoning, maybe," Harriet said dryly. "Look, I haven't got all day. Who do I have to peck into submission to get my dressmaker and business manager back?"

2 7

EVA

*E*va blinked back tears of hope and joy. She didn't care if the Queen or her court saw her cry, but she didn't want to miss a moment of the unbelievable story unfolding before her because of blurry vision.

Harriet had come to save her.

Eva knew that Bruno and Margo would fight for her, but she hadn't expected Harriet's brusque loyalty, or Tobias's faithful support. She didn't know Frank and Anita at all, except by reputation, but they were already listing the people who would come and advocate for each of them if anyone lost. "I couldn't get Frank's family here on such short notice, but with three days between each challenge, they can get standby flights from Florida and still be here before it's too late. Have you tried one of the sour apple cupcakes? Those green ones! They're one of my most popular flavors! They were Harriet's idea, really."

"I don't need that kind of credit," Harriet assured her.

The gargoyle leaned in to the Queen and if Eva had not been standing so close to her chair, she would not have heard his words.

"How much do you want these women for yourself? Enough to risk being a laughingstock as this string of misfits fight for their friends and possibly even sometimes win? How many champions do you ultimately have to throw at them?"

His gravelly voice went unexpectedly winsome. "A wise ruler would recognize an opportunity to regain respect. It would be an act of unsurpassed generosity to let them all go. Your court could use a reminder of *mercy*." He walked backwards a few steps before the Queen could answer.

Eva could feel the Queen's struggle, but the gargoyle was not wrong.

The faery monarch had greatly misjudged her court's appetite for cruelty, and she must know that she was losing her grip on them. They *wanted* to see love win over revenge and they were charmed by this show of rag-tag loyalty and friendship. Anita was already pressing cupcakes on everyone. An elegantly-dressed, stag-horned man was eating his third, and there was icing on his nose.

"Eva?" The Queen looked at the gold chain in her hands and gave it a little tug.

Eva left Margo's side, gesturing her to wait where she was, and went to her customary place at the Queen's side.

"Yes." The Queen's voice was so quiet that the word seemed like a floating flower petal out of the corner of an eye that wasn't there when you turned to look.

"Yes, what?" Eva was confused.

"You asked me if I loved you. Yes, I loved you. I couldn't stand the idea of losing you. It was more than just pride, though I know you think that's all it was. I was...I was afraid you'd leave me and I manifested my own fears by forcing you." The Queen—Katerina—drew herself up proudly. "And now, you will be the one who put me back on my own path." She snapped her fingers and the cuff at

Eva's ankle vanished with a musical tinkle with a matching chime from Margo's. "For what it's worth, I'm sorry."

"It's worth more than you might think," Eva said, and she dared to tip forward enough to kiss the Queen on her forehead. "Thank you."

She hopped from the throne and took Margo's hand in hers to dive into the milling crowd to find Bruno. They nearly ran into the bubbly little baker that had come to Faery with Frank Wilson as she came tripping forward to the dais.

"Your MAJESTY!" Anita gave a curtsy so low she almost fell over forward. "If you would honor me by accepting a cupcake!" She held it up in front of her, her head bowed.

The Queen rose to her feet and came forward to Anita, plucking the frosted treat from her hand. "I accept this offering," she said formally. And then, to everyone's amazement, she sat down on the dais to peel off the paper. "It is very *green*."

Anita plopped down beside her. "It's my own formula, top secret! Lots of citric acid, which is actually really healthy. It prevents kidney stones! I never had problems with kidney stones myself. Do fairies have kidneys? Oh, I'm sorry that's probably too personal." She showed off her verdant fingers. "The green dye is a bit of a hassle to work with, but I don't mind!"

A dryad crept forward and shyly compared finger hues with Anita, and the rest of the court gathered around as the Queen took a careful bite of her cupcake, flashing her sharp teeth as she did.

It was one of Anita's sour apple cupcakes, and Eva had to laugh at the Queen's expression of surprise and disgust.

She still chewed and swallowed, and then licked the frosting from her lips as everyone watched her anxiously.

"It is…interesting," she said diplomatically, and then she took another bite.

Bruno made it to the front of the crowd then and he grinned when saw that their shackles were gone.

"I release you," the Queen said, before he could ask. "You are all free to go. You have done enough damage here already."

Eva was scooped up into Bruno's arms and crushed against Margo.

EPILOGUE - BRUNO

There was some discussion about who would walk whom down the aisle, but in the end, Margo and Eva walked themselves, hand-in-hand.

Most of the guests were coworkers, from Harriet's bakery and from Wilson Kinetics, but a surprising contingent from Faery had also accepted invitations. There was no brides' side or groom's side, since Bruno had argued that would be an unfair advantage to the brides and that the apostrophes were too challenging for the signage.

So there were mechanics and janitors elbow-to-elbow with the Fae court. Burly blue-collared mechanics sat next to winged and antlered sprites, and Gary seemed quite taken with one of Harriet's tattooed bakers. They appeared to be comparing piercings. Bruno waited at the dais, Frank as his best man at his side. Anita was both bridesmaid and flower girl, and she told everyone that the flower petals were edible as she scattered them generously on the floor and audience. Tobias and Harriet came next, because Tobias had refused to let Harriet go down the aisle alone, even as the maid of honor.

Bruno was pretty sure that Tobias was whispering dirty suggestions to her as they walked, judging by Harriet's flush and Tobias's satisfied smirk.

Then came Eva and Margo, and Bruno could not even see anyone else for the glory of his mates.

Margo had protested wearing white. "I am a troll," she insisted. "You put me in a white suit and people will think I'm the marshmallow man from the Ghostbusters movie and the whole wedding will be screaming and fleeing. A cupcake dress would be even worse." So Eva made her a tailored feminine suit of moss green and teal blues, an earthy, watery kit with a pattern of silver leaves, dark lace, and subtle embroidery designs in the same shades of red and rust as Bruno's fitted suit.

Eva's dress was silver and gray, shot through with Margo's greens and teals and Bruno's russet hues. It had puffed sleeves and a frothy skirt, with rainbow crystals sewn into every seam. Bruno didn't realize that it left her back boldly bare until she turned a little climbing up onto the dais and he saw the flash of her raw scars.

She stood proudly before the officiant, a rather bemused-looking recruit from the civil clerk's desk and Margo faced Bruno from beside her.

The clerk cleared his throat and addressed the room.

"We are gathered here today in celebration of love and union between these three souls. Let us join them together in the presence of witnesses and wish them joy and happiness as they start a journey forward from this day as husband and wives. I understand that you have written your own vows?"

They had written their vows together, because Eva insisted that she didn't want to get up in front of everyone and say "Me, too," when she realized that everyone else had said what she was going to first.

"Bruno," Margo said first. "I fell headfirst into your life hiding from security guards and you kissed me instead of turning me in." There was a titter of amusement from the audience. "Eva, I have adored you since Harriet first introduced me to her assistant and never realized that you might look twice at me. The two of you together complete me, and I swear my heart and my soul to each of you forever."

Bruno cleared his throat and realized that he'd crushed his note cards in sweaty hands. "Eva, you came quietly into my life and stole my heart. Margo, you hit me over the head with a popcorn machine."

"My popcorn machine!" Frank whispered from behind him in outrage. "You said that was done by vandals!"

Bruno closed his eyes and dredged the rest up from memory because the ink on the index card was too smudged to read. "The two of you together complete me, and I swear my body and my being to each of you forever."

Eva was bouncing slightly in place, light as a dandelion fluff. "Margo, I will never forget how kind you were to me when I had nothing, and now you've given me everything. Bruno, I was afraid of so much when we met, and you made me feel brave again. The two of you together complete me, and I swear my love and life to each of you forever."

Eva kissed Margo, standing on tiptoe as Margo bent over, and it was a fluttery kiss full of promise, just like their very first one. Then Margo stood up and kissed Bruno, and it was a lingering kiss, pressed close together. While she caught her breath, Bruno turned to Eva and swept her into a third kiss that was barely civil, as the audience burst into applause.

The sweaty clerk shook all of their hands and looked happy to escape with a plate from the reception buffet.

There was a tower of gifts, ranging from very practical (a new stand mixer and a smoked sausage subscription) to very tongue in cheek (a boxed DVD set of Threes Company).

Bruno was alarmed to find a card from the Faery Queen (who went by Queen Katerina now) in with the gifts, but Eva opened it fearlessly.

This gift is not equal to the forgiveness you have granted me, but I hope it starts to heal the wounds that I caused.

    Love forever,

    Queen Katerina

The card had a triskelion on it that glowed in blue and then vanished as Eva gave a gasp of wonder. Bruno growled and spun, looking for some trick or trap, and found that wings had sprouted from her shoulders in glowing blue.

Margo brushed her hand through them suspiciously. They dragged like smoke along her fingers, then coalesced behind them.

"Do they hurt?" she asked.

Eva sighed in joy, turning her head to see them. "No, not at all. It's perfect."

"Well that certainly overshadows our gift," Frank said, not sounding that disappointed. He handed Eva an envelope as well. "Tobias and I, with Harriet and Anita, took care of the debt you had outstanding with Antonio."

Eva gave everyone hugs, and Bruno shook everyone's hands, and Margo even smiled.

Much later, Bruno soaked with Eva and Margo in the honeymoon suite of the fanciest hotel in the city, which was saying a lot. His huge copper tub was installed there, filled with steaming water and floating with flowers. The sale had secured his expenses for at least a year, and he had a mate and a wife on each side of him.

"You never did tell us what the Queen offered you to give up your challenge," Margo observed, dragging her fingers through the wet, curly hair on Bruno's chest.

Eva squirmed out of his embrace and sat up to stare down at him. "It made you *blush*," she pointed out. "It must have been good."

Bruno groaned and tried to slip down deeper into the tub. Even now, his ears were heating.

"Tell us!" Margo commanded, splashing him.

"Tell us!" Eva echoed, tickling him.

Bruno chortled and caught Eva under one arm as he rolled away from Margo, who followed until they were all grappling in one confusion of waves and limbs. The mat beside the tub was already soaked.

"I give up!" he finally said. "Eva's elbows are too pointy." They settled back into comfortable shapes together, warm and floaty in the bubbles and rose petals.

"What did she offer you?" Eva asked. "Unlimited riches?"

"Fame as an artist equal to Frank's?" Margo guessed.

"A lifetime of Faery food?"

"A coffee cup that never goes cold?"

"A new hammer for your next bathtub?"

Bruno sighed. "It's...sort of a tool..."

"You're blushing again," Eva pointed out.

Bruno slid down and lowered his face into the water. "Oo ox," he said into it with bubbles.

"Blue socks?" Margo puzzled over the sounds that he'd made.

Eva fell backwards laughing. "Two cocks! Of course!!"

"She could do that?" Margo said in wonder. "Really? Why wouldn't you take that offer?"

Bruno's face emerged from the water. "What would be the point if I didn't have both of you to please?"

"Butt stuff?" Eva offered innocently.

"You did *not* just say that," Margo sighed. "You know how prudish Bruno is."

"Help!" Bruno wailed, laughing so hard he nearly drowned himself. "Someone save me!"

Eva tried to pull him up by the armpit, slipped, and splashed her head under the water. Margo pulled her up like a wet kitten, and got an arm under Bruno to heave him out of the water. "Saved," she said, planting a kiss on each of their cheeks.

"You saved me long before this," Eva said, turning to capture her lips.

"You both saved me," Bruno said, low and sure. Whatever life threw at the three of them, they would face it together, stronger and better than they could ever be apart.

Hugs, his bear said happily, and that, for once, was the perfect thing to do.

A NOTE FROM ELVA BIRCH

I am definitely not writing a book for Gary the Gargoyle. I am certainly not researching garden statuary or compiling dad jokes about rocks. Please do not email these jokes to elvaherself@elvabirch.com if you trip across them. Absolutely do not subscribe to my newsletter or join my Reader's Retreat on Facebook in order to get sneak previews and snippets of this next book that I'm not actually writing…

If you enjoyed reading about a threesome, I do have one other available, The Neighbors Might Talk!

As always, your reviews are very much appreciated; I read them all and they help other readers decide whether or not to buy my books! A huge thank you to all of my amazing beta readers and copy editors; any errors that remain are entirely my own. If you find typos — or you'd just like share your thoughts with me! — please feel free to email me at elvaherself@elvabirch.com.

To find out about my new releases, you can follow me on Amazon.

A Day Care for Shifters: A steamy full-length series about adorable shifter kids and their struggling single parents in a town full of mystery and surprise. Start the series with Wolf's Instinct, when Addison comes to Nickel City to take a job at a very special day care and finds a family to belong to. A gentle ice-cream-straight-from-the-container escape. Sweet and sizzling!

The Royal Dragons of Alaska: A fascinating alternate world where Alaska is ruled by secret dragon shifters. Adventure, romance, and humor! Reluctant royalty, relentless enemies…dogs, camping, and magic! Start with The Dragon Prince of Alaska.

Suddenly Shifters: A hilarious series of novellas, serials, and shorts set in the small town of Anders Canyon, where something (in the water?) is making ordinary citizens turn into shifters. Start with Something in the Water! Also available in audio!

~

The Flamingo's Fated Mate: It was supposed to be an April Fool's joke, but turned into a sweet-hot, side-splitting romance romp. It certainly won't be a series. I'm definitely not writing a sequel. (If you want sneak previews of the sequel I'm *definitely* not writing, join my Reader's Retreat on Facebook or sign up for my newsletter at elvabirch.com!)

~

Birch Hearts: An enchanting collection of short stories and novellas. Unconstrained by theme or setting, each short read has romance, magic, and heart, with a satisfying conclusion. And always, the impossible and irresistible. Start with a sampler plate in Prompted 2 for fourteen pieces of sweet-to-sizzling flash fiction, or dive in with the novella, Better Half. Breakup is a free story!

Shifting Sands Resort: A complete ten-book series - plus two collections of shorts. This is a sizzling shifter romance set at a tropical island resort. Each book stands alone but connects into a great mystery with a thrilling conclusion. Start with Tropical Tiger Spy or dive in to the Omnibus edition, with all of the novels, short stories, and novellas in my preferred reading order! Shifting Sands Resort crosses over with **Shifter Kingdom** and **Fire and Rescue Shifters**.

~

Fae Shifter Knights: A complete four-book fantasy portal romp, with cute pets and swoon-worthy knights stuck in a world of wonders like refrigerators and ham sandwiches. Start with Dragon of Glass!

~

Green Valley Shifters: A sweet, small town series with single dads, secret shifters, sweet kids, and spinsters. Low-peril and steamy! Standalone books where you can revisit your favorite characters - this series is also complete! Start with Dancing Barefoot! Green Valley Shifters crosses over with **Virtue Shifters**. Start with Timber Wolf!

SNEAK PREVIEW: DRAGON'S INSTINCT

Shots sizzled across the speeder's bow and Turnkey dove at the controls. "We've got a problem!" he hollered back to the engineer.

"You're telling me!" Tagrin shouted back. "We've got a coolant leak in the quarterdeck and a crack in the second hull! She's not going to hold together long enough to break atmo!"

"I know how to fix this!" Turnkey said—

Jan stopped typing, his fingers poised over the laptop.

He had no *idea* how to fix this.

It had taken him twenty minutes to re-read and remember where he was even going with his plot when he sat down to write and his brain felt shattered. He couldn't recall when he'd last gotten a full night's sleep or more than an hour of writing time in one sitting. Every time that he so much as started feeling like he was making progress on his book, his toddler daughter, Lucy, needed a snack, or a new diaper, or a hug, or a nap, or it was time for a meal or to do laundry or there was a toy that needed to be repaired.

Or, like now, there was suspicious silence, which was even worse.

Ian thought he'd have a little window of writing opportunity. Lucy had been happily playing with her food at the table, and as slow as she ate, Ian guessed he might be able to get a few hundred words written.

He didn't want to think about how a few hundred words at a time wasn't going to get him finished by the publisher's (third) deadline, or how many times he'd had to delete big chunks because he was incapable of holding the whole book in his head and his plot had gone straight off the tracks.

"Lu?"

Ian leaned back in his chair so that he could see into the kitchen.

Lucy's chair was empty, and her purple butterfly dress was hanging off the back of it. It hung neatly, as if she had taken it off before she shifted.

Ian swore under his breath and cheerfully called, "Lucy? Honey? Did you finish your food?" He should have kept her in a high chair a little longer, he thought woefully. But she was tall for her age and had convinced him that she was ready for a big girl chair. She was, but was he?

The sandwich that she'd been playing with had been disassembled and all the parts she liked had been eaten out. The halved cherry tomatoes were gone, of course, they never lasted long enough to be entertainment. Her sippy cup was on its side, a few drops of water on the table beneath it.

"Lucy, you know I don't want to play hide and seek right now. Lucy?"

Ian was equal parts annoyed and worried. There was so much trouble that a little girl could get into...and even more that a squirrel could. She'd been so safely occupied, and he'd barely looked away. He was the worst dad, he was a miserable failure, how hard could it be to juggle a stay-at-home career and one small child?

Pretty damned hard, it turned out. Ian scanned the top of the fridge and the cabinets in the kitchen; Lucy liked high places. But she wasn't in any of her usual spots, and Ian spread his search zone down the hall. "Lucy, please come out. Honey, are we playing a game? You know that Daddy needs to get his book finished, but if you want me to, I can read you one of *your* books. Lucy?"

The carpet gave a suspicious squelch, right in front of the bathroom and Ian flung the door open to find that there was water in a shallow pool all across the floor. "Argh!" He was wearing socks, and they were immediately soaked as he dashed across to the sink, where the tap was still running. There was a washcloth lying across the bottom of the bowl and when Ian pulled it out, the water in the bowl swiftly drained away. A few water-logged dolls sagged at the bottom.

"Lucy!!"

Ian made himself temper his voice. Lucy had probably realized that she'd done something wrong and was hiding as a squirrel in one of the million tiny places in this house where he'd never find her.

"Lucy, you aren't in trouble," he called as gently as he could. "I just need to know that you're okay!"

He pulled the towels down off the rack to start sopping up the puddle. He had a box fan somewhere, he'd better get it going in the hallway before they had a mold problem to add to the mix.

The phone rang while he was wringing out the towels for the second time. "Hang on," he said when the fan drowned out the caller.

"You sound like you're in an air tunnel," Wanda

complained when he got the fan turned off. When Ian was feeling his most lonely and full of regret over their broken relationship, she usually managed to say just the right thing to remind him why they'd parted ways.

"Sorry," he said, knowing he didn't sound sorry. "What's up?"

"I wanted to talk about The Schedule."

She always said it like both words were capitalized.

The Schedule.

The Schedule was the calendar that dictated the days they had to see each other, the days that Lucy was hers or his. At first, Wanda had been adamant about getting every day allotted to her with their joint custody, and Ian had spent the days she was gone desperately missing his daughter. But Wanda got busier with work, her new boyfriend had kids, and Wanda had gradually adjusted The Schedule so that Ian had Lucy nearly all the time. He'd even thought about pressuring her for child support, but it had never felt like he was equal to the effort.

"After all," she'd said more than once. "You don't work, it's not an inconvenience to you."

Ian wasn't sure which part of her assumption he objected to most. That writing wasn't working? That raising a small child basically by himself wasn't a whole job all by itself? But like most battles with Wanda, it simply wasn't worth fighting anymore.

"What about it?" Ian sounded more surly than he meant. Was she going to want to talk to Lucy? Did he have to admit that he didn't know where she was and that she'd just flooded the bathroom?

Wanda sounded almost sweet. "I know I said I didn't want any of the holidays this year, but my parents invited us up to Helena for Labor Day. They'd like to see Lucy."

Ian remembered holidays with Wanda's folks. They

were all squirrel shifters, and while he adored his daughter beyond reason, the ceaseless chattering and the way Wanda's family was always in constant motion always left him feeling like he'd been in a room full of mental vampires after only a few minutes. Having to stay with them had been a kind of fine-tuned torture.

Labor Day. "Let me check my calendar."

Ian didn't really have to look at it. Aside from the looming red BOOK DUE (really, this time!) entry on his calendar, it was just a trudging list of nothing. The closest he'd gotten to a social life lately was babysitting his friend Roderick's daughter Gabby, a little girl just younger than Lucy, while Roderick took his new girlfriend out on a date.

Sometimes, it seemed like everyone was moving on without him.

"That should work fine," Ian said.

"You're a peach," Wanda said sunnily. "I'll pick her up that Saturday morning and drop her off on Monday evening. Let me talk to Lucy."

Dammit.

"Hang on." He muted the phone, double-checking that he had, and then hollered, "Lucy! Come talk to your mom! She's on the phone *right now!*"

A rustle at the baseboard gave him a few seconds of warning, and then Lucy shot out from behind the heater, her rusty red fur covered in dust.

She flowed up into a little girl, completely naked, and reached grabby hands for the phone.

"I'll hold it for you, honey," Ian said, thumbing the connection back on. He knew there were parents that would casually hand children Lucy's age a several hundred dollar phone—Wanda among them—but he didn't trust her attention span and he couldn't afford to replace it.

"Mummy! Bathroom's all wet!"

Ian couldn't hear Wanda's answer to that, and he oversaw half of a halting conversation before Lucy agreed, "Kisses!" and waved at the phone.

Ian checked to see that Wanda had hung up and put the phone back in his pocket. "You want to tell me about the bathroom?" he asked.

Lucy eyed her escape route back under the heater and Ian made a note to try to block it up with something. His entire house had become an obstacle course of trying to keep her out of small places and dangerous things. The cabinet locks were a constant frustration, as much for him as they were for her, and she could climb *anything*.

"You're not in trouble," Ian promised. "I just want to make sure it doesn't happen again, honey."

She wilted and mumbled something about dolls, carrots, and possibly a trombone.

"Just make sure you ask me before you play in the bath-room," Ian begged. "And turn off the water. We don't want to waste it!"

Lucy looked up at him hopefully, then said, "I'm hungry."

It was her get-out-jail-free card. Ian wasn't going to deny her *food*, no matter how recently she'd eaten, and he bent and scooped her up into his arms. "What did you forget, sweety?"

Lucy put two fingers in her mouth and said, "Clothes?" around them.

"Clothes," Ian agreed. "You're supposed to take your clothes with you when you shift."

Ian found himself at eye level with the business card magnet that Roderick had given him the week before as he opened the fridge. Cherry's new day care for shifter chil-dren, Tiny Paws, apparently taught kids to shift with their clothing.

A day care for shifter children.

Maybe he could talk Wanda into helping to pay for it. Maybe, if he could finish his damned book, he could pay for it himself. It would be good for Lucy to get more socialization. He couldn't just go set up playdates with the neighborhood kids when she was so good at shifting and so terrible about knowing when she was supposed to.

"Do you want a yogurt squeezie?" Ian offered. He knew she would.

When he put her down for a protesting nap, an hour later, he went back to his laptop. There were sticky squirrel footprints on the lid.

I know how to fix this, he thought hopefully.

He opened up his phone and punched in the number for Tiny Paws.

"Hi," he said when Cherry answered. "I was wondering if you had any openings…"

❧

*I*an's got enough problems being a single dad to a squirrel-shifting toddler…even before she starts breathing fire and gets caught by the new neighbor's cat. Fortunately, A Day Care for Shifters is there to save the day!

www.ingramcontent.com/pod-product-compliance
Lightning Source LLC
Chambersburg PA
CBHW061536120726
48001CB00004B/1583